MY TRIP TO MARDI GRAS

And Other Stories

HENRY CHOICE

C H A P T E R   1

The Beginning

Have you ever noticed that kids do dumbass things? It is necessary for their development. If they don't make any mistakes, then they aren't learning some very powerful lessons in life. If you listen to everything that you are told from people more experienced than you and don't make the same mistakes that others before you have made, what have you learned? The lessons you learn from making mistakes teach you why you shouldn't behave a certain way, but they also teach you that others are looking after you by telling you what not to do. The lessons are stronger, and you gain wisdom when you do it the hard way.

I was standing on the interstate in Birmingham, Alabama, at three o'clock in the morning. I had been dropped off there by a van filled with the most thieves I had ever been associated with. It was April, and I suppose you could say it was typical middle-of-the-night weather for the south. I had a jacket on and felt comfortable, probably because there was no wind to speak of. You wouldn't think an interstate would be deserted, but this one was. I'll bet I was there ten or fifteen minutes without seeing one solitary vehicle. Normally, at least half of the cars that go by wouldn't offer a ride to a hitchhiker. At that rate, I wouldn't get a ride for hours.

The first car that did come by was a station wagon that was at least ten years old. Surprisingly, the driver pulled over. He had a beard and fairly long brown hair.

"Hey, how ya doin'?" I said. Sometimes going with the classics in a greeting situation is like gold. All right, I guess I could have said something more memorable, but sometimes, it's just not there.

"Good enough. I'm Bobby. Where are you heading?" he replied.

"I'm Henry, and I'm going to New Orleans."

"That's good enough, because that's where I'm headed."

I felt like I was doing the right thing. I had just spent about three weeks driving through Florida in a stolen van with a pack of thieves. I liked them. They were my friends. But I was getting too paranoid with them. I was heading back to a place I hoped would be home for a while. I had been traveling around, mostly hitchhiking, for almost eight months, and it was not as cool as it had been when I had started. I was tired of the road, and I was ready to do something else—like live in a house. I was also headed toward a girl. Girls sure do know how to get into your head.

Why did I feel like I was doing something right? Because karma was pointing me that direction. I know. Karma? What the fuck am I talking about, right?

Well, this ride, for instance. I was put out on the interstate in the middle of the night, and the first ride that came along was going to take me within a block of my destination. How about the fact that he had a bag full of different kinds of pot? How about the fact that I rolled up a couple of joints from a couple of bags and we got perfectly stoned? How about the fact that we had a good conversation while we cruised down an empty interstate, wasted, on a nice, early springtime morning? It's not often that you get things to line up to be a real good day. It's like I made a decision and all the circumstances told me that it would indeed be a great day. Whether these things were a reward for making a good decision or not, it made me feel that it was right.

After a couple hours, Bobby suggested I get in the back of the station wagon and nod off for a while. So I did. Too bad I missed the sunrise. Sunrises are always interesting when you're stoned.

Bobby let me off by the Hare Krishna temple on Esplanade between Broad and City Park. I walked a block over to Desoto and then two houses over to 3211. I walked up the steps to the porch and looked at four doors. The door on the far left was the entrance to an apartment on the first floor on the left. The second led to the upstairs on the left. The third door was for the upstairs on the right, and the fourth was for the downstairs apartment. I opened the second from the right.

As I started up the stairs, Jonnie came running to the top. She was smiling. No, that's definitely not an accurate description of the look on her face. She looked like she was seeing something that she had wanted but had told herself she wasn't going to get. In my thirty-six years of marriage to her, I don't believe I've ever seen her as glad to see me as she was that day. I don't care who you are; having somebody glad to see you is one of the good things in life.

I walked up the stairs and into another part of my life.

When a man hits his groove in life, where he is doing the same thing for years—sometimes known as his rut—he gets to thinking about the paths he took. Once your life has hit that halfway point, once you are looking at a shorter time ahead than there was behind, you are probably looking at the decisions that landed you where you are. I don't think that anyone can say that there was only one decision that put him where he is. Usually, though, there is one decision that changes one's life and points one in the direction of this life more than any other. For most people, it happens when they're young and flexible enough to accept and flow with the change.

My daughter got me thinking a lot about it lately, because she was asking me about some of the things I did after high school before I met her mom. I have told a lot of people some of what happened during that time, but I haven't told the whole story. One day, I know my memory will be shot and the story will be lost. I'm afraid that day will come before I'm ready for it to be here. Anyway, I figured that it was a story that might be worth telling.

I suppose my trip started in October of '71. After a football game, I was in the process of buying beer at the local Quick Stop when my cross-country coach decided to pull up front so that his wife could come in and buy some milk. My friends Kirk and Lonnie and I told the cashier to stash the beer behind the counter as we proceeded to wait for their departure. Of course, it wasn't too obvious that we'd been caught in the act of doing something wrong. We were standing behind the magazine rack and looking over the top, obviously waiting for him to leave. After you have been teaching awhile, you get to where you know something's going on by the looks on kids' faces.

Coach had been teaching for awhile, so he pretty well put two and two together. On Monday, he proceeded to investigate by asking the biggest drunk on the team if he knew if anyone on the team was drinking. My teammate already knew about the incident, so he naturally replied, "No, Coach." Coach never did like me much after that. I tend to think he overreacted. I see him and talk to him from time to time nowadays because he and my dad go fishing together and hang out.

I didn't feel much like drinking beer that night, even after going to the trouble of buying it—and in those days, it was trouble for a teenager to buy beer. I had a beer or two, but I was in a slightly melancholy mood and didn't drink much. I don't think the incident at the Quick Stop was the reason behind the mood, but the mood did transfer to the next day.

The next day was the start of my biggest single decision: we seniors went to take the ACT at the local college. At first, I took the test seriously and did well. Along about the third section of the test, my melancholy from the previous night took hold in the form of apathy. I distinctly remember looking around at the other students and not feeling like doing anything. That's a common characteristic of teenagers. They don't think about the consequences; they just follow the whim of their newly developing emotions. They don't understand what it is that they are feeling, so they just shut down. That's one of the reasons no one can stand a teenager except another teenager, and even that's a risky proposition. Later, I got my test results. I got a 25 on one test, a 29 in math, but then a 16 and a 17 on the last two tests.

As I walked out and sat down in my light-blue, '58 Chevrolet Delray, I knew I had botched part of the test due to my uncontrolled mood. I said, "Oh, well. I didn't want to go to college anyway." I didn't mean it when I said it. My parents and I had always assumed that I was going to college, and it was like that for everybody I knew. It was just a joking comment I made to cover up the situation.

I don't know how long it took to sink in, but somehow, it sank. I did not want to go to college. I don't believe I set my mind on it that day, but I never turned back from that feeling again that year.

Now is the time in the story where I tell you that you wouldn't be able to truly understand the story if you didn't know the background. So let's get on with it. I came from the plains of the Midwest. The plains can have their beauty. The gently rolling topography with fields of wheat and other crops are decorated with fifteen- to twenty-foot-high hedgerows. In the 1930s, they were planted every half mile to fight off the dust storms of the Depression. When you are traveling through the plains, you can tell when you are coming upon a town or a creek because you'll start to see a lot of trees. The plains are almost heavily forested in comparison to how they were when people first started living in and developing the area.

My hometown is an affluent little community of twelve to fifteen thousand people. I'm not saying it was a wealthy community, such as Hyannis Port or Newport, but for a community its size, it had a disproportionate number of rich people without very many poor people. There are probably more millionaires in town than people on welfare. The town didn't suffer much during the Depression, as the story goes, because the oil fields in the area were discovered and developed during the twenties and thirties. The town also had a refinery. I used to think that the movie *Splendor in the Grass* with Natalie Wood and Warren Beatty was written about my hometown.

That prosperity has never changed, because to this day, besides the refinery, the town includes four fairly large plastic plants, an insulation plant, and a drug company. The only way not to have a job is not to want one. Everybody has a job, and those companies contribute a lot of cash to the community in terms of donations and taxes. The parks and the schools are beautiful and well maintained. The streets and roads are well planned, built, and maintained. There weren't then, and aren't now, many dilapidated or abandoned houses in town.

Just to let you know the makeup of the town, the year I graduated, there were five black males but no black females and no other minorities in the school. For the most part, the black kids didn't act any different, because they grew up around us. When Billy Jackson, the only black kid in my elementary school, was taking a piss back in 1961 and I looked at his dick, I didn't think that he should be in his own school. I was just surprised that he wasn't circumcised. For years, I thought that all black kids had weird dicks.

Now, am I saying that having five black males and no black females didn't cause some problems? No, indeed not. Luke Marshall, who was our all-state football and basketball player, went off to the college of his choice, and I'm not sure if he ever had a date all through high school. That must have been one hell of a pain in the ass. We were the picture of a white middle-class, American community. Hell, Beaver Cleaver could have been from this town.

There's also a thing called the Midwest morality and work ethic. People went to work and did their jobs because that's what you did in that time and place. Little girls stayed virgins longer. When people did stray from accepted group norms in the form of thievery, laziness, drugs, or easy virtue, then the old folks would say to each other in a low voice, "You know, Joe has no job and is on drugs. I also hear that his sister fucks a lot of different guys." This statement, without a doubt, would be accompanied by a head lowered and shaken from side to side in the universal look of disapproval, as if it was an exclamation point to the severity of not conforming to the code of behavior. The other old folks would agree with the statement and the inappropriateness of the behavior by shaking their heads with frowns on their faces.

Unfortunately, as wise and responsible as this attitude is, it has its drawbacks. If you aren't having any fun in your life, then what's the point? While it seems that the spice cabinet of any good Midwestern home has both salt and pepper, the cook needs to be careful with the pepper, because it has a kick. I think people should put some spice in their lives. I wanted some spice in my life, but I didn't know what it was that I was missing. I just knew there had to be something else. I also knew that it was not a good idea to try my spice in my hometown. Not only was there not enough spice in that little town, but I also didn't want the town elders looking at me, talking about how I was using too much spice, and shaking their heads in disapproval.

There had to be good and bad. If all you know is good, how can you tell if that's better? Everybody has to have bad times so that they'll know when the good times are there. It probably does make sense to follow the rules and advice of one's elders, but I believe everyone should do something in his or her life that is contrary to what the elders told them, just so they can see why. Everyone should go too far at least once, just so they know how far is too far.

For the next few months, I don't believe I thought about my decision much. If I did, it was just to confirm in my mind the decision I had made. Mostly, I went about the business of being a senior. I went to parties, did the minimum amount of work to graduate, and played a lot of sports. I coached a fourth-grade basketball team, played basketball on a church league team, and played front-yard football or hockey on the creek on Saturdays.

The time did come for me to make a permanent decision, though. I came home from somewhere about ten on a weeknight in March or

April. I went into the den, which was past the living room where my mom was. She asked me if I had applied to any colleges or anything. I must have pretty well made my mind up, because I said, "I don't think I want to go to college."

My mom was pretty forceful about what she wanted, and she had it in her mind that her kids were going to get a better opportunity for their futures than she'd had. That was the great American dream for that generation, who had grown up during the Depression and went through the biggest war in history before they hit thirty. They were tough because they were forced to be, but like most parents, they wanted their kids to have it better than they did. After all, they were leading America into the most prosperous times that any nation in the history of man had achieved. So they felt they had a right to expect their children to conform to what they knew was best for them. Unfortunately, when we're children, it's our duty to break up our parents' dreams so that we can say we led our lives. Teenagers have to cut the ropes to get on their own and be independent.

As for my mom, we didn't usually like to cross her. I never will forget the look on her face at that moment. Her face tightened up, especially her mouth. Her eyebrows were down and serious. Let me tell you, that glare had some heat. What she said next sort of sealed the deal. She said, "I have a good mind to *make* you go!"

To my credit, I did not say anything. Maybe I was thinking about how she was going to accomplish that. There's an old saying that I always thought applied well to this situation: "You can lead a horse to water, but you can't make him drink." As a teacher, I know that you cannot make a person learn if he doesn't want to. I believe that we both knew when she said it that it wasn't very enforceable. I went to bed.

A few days later, my dad asked me at the dinner table if it was true that I wasn't planning to go to college. Obviously, my mom had had a talk with him and probably wanted him to talk to me. He wasn't normally the one to do much of the raising of the kids, so I figure she put him up to it. In my family, the jobs of the parental units were clearly defined, as they were in most families during that time. The father worked every day at a job so that he could provide the money, and the mother took care of the kids, and since she had to do it every day, she got to make up the rules and such. My dad's main job when it came to the kids was to provide backup. My two brothers, my sister, and I all knew that whatever my mom decided, my dad would be standing right behind her. I believe I only got one spanking from my dad. On the third day that I didn't hang up my coat in the closet, my dad followed me into the closet, turned me upside down by my feet, and gave me a spanking. I was too shocked to cry. I never doubted that my dad fully intended to back up what he told us to.

One time, I was in the process of playing the "in a minute/I forgot" game with my mom. After dinner one evening, after my mom had cleaned the kitchen, she told me to take out the trash. At this time, I went ahead and stated the customary "in a minute" statement because, after all, I was watching a very important episode of Quick Draw McGraw. Of course, I was planning on telling her, "I forgot" the next morning. It had worked quite well a few times in the past. Maybe I had gone to that well one too many times, because my dad then said, "Didn't your mother tell you to do something?" I decided to go take out the trash right then rather than wait for a commercial. As a rule, though, my dad didn't take an active part in the everyday raising of us little urchins.

Back to my dad's conversation at the table: I told him yeah, I'd decided I wasn't going to college. He asked me what I planned on doing. I don't remember having it firm in my mind until that moment, but when I told him that I wanted to travel, I knew that that was true and that I wanted it a lot.

After that time, whenever anyone young asked me where I was going to school, I said I was going to Australia University on a kangaroo wrestling scholarship. For those of you who know me now, see, I've always been "out there." I had it in my mind that I wanted to go to Australia. I'm not sure where I got the idea, but by summertime, it was firmly set in my mind that that is what I wanted to do.

Over a couple of days when I was in eighth grade, we took some tests that asked a lot of weird questions. The next year, in civics class while we were researching what we wanted to do when we grew up, we got the results of that test, which was designed to lead us toward a career that would fit our interests and our strengths. My results heavily favored the writing side of me. It was suggested that I go into law, which has a high verbal and writing content, or just plain be a writer of some sort. These sorts of tests are not a bad idea, in that they are trying to get of bunch of teenagers to start thinking about what they want to do; however, their results cannot be taken as the answer. I soon found out the law was not a good choice, because when I took debate in high school, I found out I was a terrible debater. I wasn't bad at understanding the arguments or coming up with logical responses. My problem was that my logical response usually came to me two hours to three days later. Anyway, I figured that traveling would go well with being a writer. It was a good idea to get some good experiences so that I could write about it, but for some reason, I wouldn't write anything. I wrote a little bit in a notebook a few times, but I wasn't consistent about it. You really need to be the type of person who loves to write just for the fun of it.

Since I had made up my mind that I was not going to college and was going to do something different, I felt that I needed experience in a variety of ways. So that spring, I smoked marijuana—otherwise referred to as pot, weed, and Mary Jane—for the first time. I fell in love with Mary Jane. People say that marijuana leads to harder drugs, and in a way, they are right. Most people that do harder stuff start with marijuana. Does that mean that everyone that smokes pot is going to be shooting up the big horse, also known as heroin? No, I say. But once you have crossed the illegal line, it doesn't make much of a difference from a legal standpoint. Speaking of doing harder drugs, I also took my first hit of LSD that summer.

Bryan, Kirk, and Rusty got hold of some acid and decided we were going to make a special evening of going up to the lake, bringing Rusty's canoe, and having a mellow high for Kirk's and my first time. I had heard a lot about acid. Some of it was just plain false information, but most of the time, someone who has done acid can't describe what it's like. A friend of mine once showed me his psychology book that showed the webs of spiders that had been given some drugs. First, there was a normal web that wasn't perfect, but for the most part, there was a plan. Second, it showed a web that had been made after the spider had had some caffeine, and it was a wreck. The web was made all helter-skelter, with strings going every which way. The third was a web that had been made after the spider had been given LSD, and it was damn near perfect with not one string out of place. I don't think that story has any pertinence to the story I'm telling, but I always thought it was interesting.

Timothy Leary, the famous Harvard professor that sort of got this acid thing kicked off and changed his whole life because of it, used to believe that acid was intended to expand your mind and that people should take it to get in touch with their spiritual selves. Now, I don't know about that stuff, but I do know that it is some dangerous shit. If a person takes too much of it and is in a situation that is stressful or just plain fucked up, he or she can go at least temporarily crazy. I'm sure a lot of you have heard of that urban legend about the guy at Woodstock who was injected with LSD 25, which is supposed to be pure LSD, and has been in a mental institution ever since; however, our first time was the type of situation that ol' Timothy would have been proud of.

So anyway, we got up to the lake out in the prairie where I was living. There are no naturally occurring lakes on the prairie. This lake was a reservoir provided by a dam. We decided to camp out by a little pond that was on the other side of the main road, about a half mile from the big lake. Before we left, we had tied the canoe to the top of Bryan's car with a blanket between it and the canoe. The canoe was a two-seat fiberglass job that Rusty had made because he thought he would like to have one. Rusty was a smart motherfucker, as was his dad, so they were always doing shit like that. He had long blonde hair down past his shoulders, but he was a little bit mushy physically. You wouldn't exactly call him fat, but he was a little overweight, and he hadn't participated in a lot of sports—or any type of exercise, for that matter. He looked about the same as about 30 percent of today's teenagers look.

In just about every high school, and in modern society, maybe even more in junior high schools, there are two main groups. They're called "jocks and hoods" or "frats and outsiders" or something similar. Now, not everyone can fit into one of these groups solidly. Often, youngsters want to fit into the elite group but are not allowed to because they're not cool enough, or they don't fit into the other group because they're not badass enough. Anyway, Rusty was in a bit of a separate group that was sort of intellectual. He and a few others were on the debate team, had very smart parents, and were content to follow their own drummers. By the time we had hit our senior year, the strict grouping that had been formalized in our earlier years was becoming muddled. A lot of the same people were going to parties in both groups. By then, some people belonged to more than one group, while others didn't belong to any.

After we took the canoe off the car, we took the acid. Whenever anyone went to sell you some acid in those days, they would make it in a variety of ways, but they would describe it to you with the name. What we had was "Orange Sunshine." See how the name makes it sound nice? Surely you would have to have a mellow trip with orange sunshine. I suppose the most famous kind of acid is Purple Haze, although I'm not really sure what made it so famous.

Bryan was low on gas when we got there and was worried that he wouldn't have enough to get back to town. So he and Kirk went to get gas, because they thought it would be easier to find a station then than in the morning. The lake was out in the sticks. There were just a few stores right around the lake and a really small town about five miles away. It turned out that they couldn't find any gas around the lake or at the small town, which didn't surprise me. So, they went to another town about fifteen miles away and couldn't find any gas there either, which I don't understand. As it turns out, they went all they way back to town to get gas so that they would have enough gas to get back to town in the morning. You know what? I think they were fucked up. And they talk about drunk drivers.

Anyway, as the sun was setting over the hill with very few clouds, Rusty and I were in a canoe on a relatively cool pond after a hot summer day, feeling no pain. I loved that canoe that night. Thinking back on that night makes me want to build my own canoe. The pond was so smooth. I wanted to say it was smooth as silk, but that phrase is a bit worn out. The problem is that I don't feel I have the capabilities to describe the euphoric sensation I was getting as the LSD was coursing through my veins and we paddled so effortlessly across the pond, feeling the breeze of the evening and watching the vibrant colors enhanced by the acid as the sun set in the west. Yeah, I know, you've all had similar experiences, so no big deal.

I don't quite recall whether it took Bryan and Kirk a couple or several hours to get back. Once they made it back, we all settled down to enjoying the feel of a summer night after a hot day, enjoying the setting, and enjoying life. We were cruising through the night on a trip that went a long way, but we never left that field that we were camped in. (I apologize if that sounds corny.)

In the wee hours of the morning, we fell into that state of mind that often happens, but usually with mushrooms, when everything is so damn funny. We started talking about a girl who was just a year younger than us and was famous for her beauty. We started talking about wanting to make a pussy sandwich or maybe have a nice, thick, juicy pussy steak. Every new variation off of that theme resulted in us going hysterical with laughter, complete with tears and sore sides. I thought I had a really good time the first time I took acid. It was definitely mellow. Maybe it was spiritual.

Before I actually go into the story of my travels, I need to lay out the story of my sexuality. No, I wasn't gay, nor did I have some embarrassing fetish. My disease, which many of us find traumatic at that time in our lives, was the disease of virginity. It took me until my senior year to finally get up the courage to ask a girl out. I spent most of my time with my girlfriend trying to cure my disease but had no real luck. If some of you remember those times, the Midwest was still trying to hang onto the old concepts. Free sex was not acceptable. Good girls didn't do it until they were old enough to understand the consequences of the act which was preferably when they were married. In those days, there was no foul language on TV. Movies were just then beginning to show sex. Gay people stayed in the closet. When a girl became pregnant while still in school, she just disappeared. One day in German class, the teacher asked who was absent, and when Johnnie said Sallie was, everyone told him to shut up, because she was gone. Later, we found out she was pregnant. When I think about how much more teenagers know about sex now compared to what we knew back then, it blows my mind.

My frustration over being a virgin was made worse by Annie. Annie was ten years older than me, lived next door, had three children, and was married. I thought she was beautiful. She had long blonde hair that she wore up most of the time. She always wore nice clothes and seemed very classy. Right after I graduated, we moved out of the house that we had lived in for twelve years and moved to a smaller but better house on the north side of town. We were no longer Annie's neighbors. It was a step up. One evening when I came home from work, Annie and Bill, her husband, were over at the house having a few drinks with my parents. The four of them were planning to go out that night.

After I had taken a shower, I went into the dining room where my parents, Annie, and Bill were. Annie was lit and begged me to let her do my hair. I had just started to let it grow. I said okay not because I wanted my hair done, but because she wanted to do it and it gave me a chance to be near her. She took me into the bathroom and proceeded to tease my hair. Remember, she was a child of the early sixties, when every good hairdo involved some teasing. After she had made my hair all puffy and combed it out, she gave me a hug and a kiss so that I could feel the alcohol in her. My mind was racing.

Of course, my dad was getting pretty lit by that time, and he chose to start calling me Puffy, which also happened to be the name of our dog. I decided that was a good time for me to leave. I went over to the funeral home where Kirk worked and told him about the whole ordeal. Kirk knew who Annie was because he worked from time to time with Bill and agreed with my assessment of her sexiness.

We had planned to go to the drive-in that night with a couple of girls that we always hung out with. Danielle and Jerri were nice-looking, fun girls, but for some reason, they were just friends, even though I thought Jerri was hot. Neither of them found me sexy enough to help me out with my disease, even though I had let it be known that I was willing, so we just ended up hanging out together.

After we left the drive-in, we decided to go to the only restaurant open at that hour in our little hick town. As we were sitting in a booth in the front part of the restaurant, across from some guys that I knew, here came my parents, Annie, and Bill, and they were past lit and into wasted. Annie saw me when they came in and said quite loudly, "There's Henry." She then proceeded to run over and give me a big kiss. She was immediately followed by my parents so that my mom could try to pry Annie away from me and my dad could start calling me Puffy while pulling on my hair. Bill just stood there and watched. Ask me if I was embarrassed. Yes, I was. In fact, I was a very deep shade of red that was accenuated by my fair WASP complexion. Even though I was I was into the seventh shade of red and extremely embarrassed, I loved the fact that Annie chose me to lay her affections on. It was a dream that had all sorts of possibilities. Too bad I didn't know how to engage those possibilities. Nothing ever happened between Annie and me.

To top off the night, when I got home and in bed, the phone rang. It was Kirk's dad, who decided to call at two in the morning to yell at me for putting shoe prints on the inside of the windshield of his car. I was confused, because I didn't remember doing that. Come to think of it, that was the night before we went to the lake. Needless to say, my head was spinning.

Alice Cooper was holding a concert in the big town down the road that summer. I wanted to go to it, but it was on a Wednesday night, and I knew my mom wouldn't go for it because I still needed to be in bed at a reasonable hour so that I could go to work. The first night that I had gotten really stoned on pot, I called home and told my mom that I was going to stay at Matt's house, and she said no because I had to go to work the next day. So I moved out. It didn't last long.

A guy I had just met had two friends move out of his apartment and needed a roommate. He also ended up moving back home two weeks later. The apartment was downtown on the second story above an old store. It used to be the police station twenty years before. The guy that owned the place rented it out to someone else before I had a chance to talk to him about it. So then, I stayed a couple of weeks with Ned while his parents were out of town.

Getting back to Alice Cooper, he had a song about being eighteen. It described quite well how I felt at the time. "I got to get out of this place" seemed to be my anthem. You can be from the absolute best place in the world, but if you don't get away from there, you'll never know it's the best place in the world. If you don't have some bad times, you won't know when you're having good times.

I went back home for a couple of weeks. One evening, my parents went up the road about thirty miles to eat with another couple, and Mom came back with a backpack for me. I was surprised. I knew at that moment that she was willing to let me go my own way.

Time to Hit the Road, or Go West, Young Man

It was about nine o'clock on a Monday morning late in August when my mom drove me out to the interstate about a mile east of town. There wasn't a cloud in the sky, and it was bright. It wasn't extremely hot out yet, but it was August, so it wasn't exactly perfect out.

My mom got out of the car with me, and I took my backpack that she had bought for me out of the back. She gave me an abbreviated look that wasn't supposed to be able to give much away but at the same time told plenty because the feelings were too close to the surface. She gave me a little hug and said good-bye and told me to write every week. Then she said lightly, or should I say, whispered that she loved me. In my family, when you said that out loud for someone to hear, even if it was a whisper, that you loved them, it was very loud. I know that that moment was one of the hardest moments of her life, but I don't think I will ever know how hard. Many mothers back then, and most mothers nowadays, wouldn't have done what she did. I'll bet that if she would have known what I was headed for, she wouldn't have done it either. I'm proud of her for that day.

She got into our old Ford station wagon with the imitation wood paneling on the side and drove to the west toward town. From the top of the overpass, I could see quite a ways in all directions. I knew it was the last time I would see the only place I had ever lived for a while. I knew this was a big day in my life, but I couldn't absorb it all. I walked over to the on-ramp to the interstate heading north and stuck out my thumb like I had seen on TV, but had never actually done.

I was going to California, but first I was going to State U that my friends were going to so that I could practice the traveling thing and give a final farewell to my friends that I had known for so long, a couple since kindergarten. It's possible that I may have been stalling.

I stayed about a week at the university. Over the weekend, Dave, Bill, Melanie, and I decided to hitchhike to a state park about a hundred miles to the north. We split up into two groups and met at the park later that afternoon. I was with Bill, and Dave was with Melanie. I was jealous because I had always had a thing for Melanie, but then again, every guy I knew had a thing for Melanie. She was so popular that she was going out with two guys during our senior year, and they both knew about it, and she got away with it. We all thought it was disgraceful but would all have jumped into the rotation without hesitating. Maybe sharing her was better than not having her at all. Maybe I'm exaggerating, and I hope I am. I saw her a couple of years ago, and it's a shame that she still is beautiful and hot at fifty-five. It doesn't quite seem fair.

When we got to the campsite, we started a fire, warmed up a can of stew, and tried roasting some field corn that one of us had picked out of a field on the way. We then analyzed the fuck out of our experience. We talked about the conversations we'd had, or lack of. Some of the people that had picked us up had been hard to talk to, and some of the conversations just flowed. We had experienced something new, and it was great. Hitchhiking could be, and was, quite often, a great way for a person to see, meet, and talk to different people. We should make politicians hitchhike across the country and meet people before they run for office. That way, they would think like other people think.

At some point, it was time to do it. I was going to start hitchhiking toward the West Coast. On my own! I was either very brave or too ignorant to know what I was getting into. Even though I like to think it was bravery, I tend to think it was the latter.

I was finishing up my first summer of smoking pot. Sometime earlier, I had purchased my first bag of real Mary Jane. Quite often back then, you ended up buying some homegrown that you usually had to smoke a great deal of to catch a buzz. Most of the time, it just stunk up the place. My stuff was supposed to be from Columbia, and I know now that most people selling the stuff are going to tell you it comes from somewhere exotic so that you will think it's something better, but that doesn't necessarily mean it comes from there. Drug dealers know that if you have someone convinced it's good stuff before you try it, the battle's halfway won. There is a huge mental aspect to drugs. Wherever my pot came from, I know it did a quite adequate job of getting me wasted. Since I was inexperienced, a little bit went a long way. After having it for at least a month and a half, I still had a substantial amount left. When I got ready to go, I rolled up a couple of joints and sold the rest.

After awhile, every hitchhiker knows that some rides leave no real lasting impression on you. You don't remember anything about the conversation or remember the face or car. But some of them do. The first ride that I will never forget happened in the capital of our fair state. The ride that landed me there was nothing of importance. I don't even remember anything about it.

I was standing on a fairly busy on-ramp in the middle of town. When I got into the late-model Ford in the middle of the morning, the first thing I saw was a *Penthouse* open on the bench seat to a picture of two beautiful women making love, and I must admit, it was tantalizing. The driver had medium-length, slightly blond hair, was in his mid thirties, and had a little mustache. My first thought was, *Salesman*. He said, quite nonchalantly, "I was about to pop a nut when I picked you up." I found it quite surprising when he said that to me, because most people I knew would not have been comfortable telling someone that they were in the process of masturbating when they decided to pick you up. I personally didn't even like to admit that I masturbated at all. I wasn't sure that he'd said and meant what I thought he had. Then the man then decided it was okay to start stroking his dick through his pant leg while commenting, "That's got to be a waste of good pussy to have them fucking each other."

Needless to say, I started to feel a great desire to polish the door handle next to me. Looking back, I now realize the guy might have been looking to pick up someone to do the job for him. I didn't realize that at the time, which was a good thing, because then I really would have felt awkward. Eventually, he finished the job himself before the ride was over. We went about fifteen or twenty miles and then he dropped me off at some desolate on-ramp out in the middle of nowhere.

I stood on the on-ramp for about fifteen minutes without anybody going by before I decided to walk up on the interstate to do my hitchhiking. So there I was, standing on the interstate hitchhiking, which was against the law, when a state trooper came cruising toward me. That panicked me, because the two joints I had rolled up earlier were taped to the inside of my cap. I immediately took off my cap, pulled out the joints, and threw them into the grass by the side of the highway. Of course, the troopers went right on by. I looked around, but I never did find the joints. I then said good-bye to the last of the first good pot I ever owned.

A hundred miles down the road, I was picked up by a trucker. It was the only time I was ever picked up by a trucker, because trucking companies forbid them to pick up hitchhikers. I think he got tired of driving everywhere alone. We stopped for lunch at some truck stop, and the man paid for my lunch. I told him it wasn't necessary, but he insisted. It wasn't because he wanted something from me, but because he just wanted to do something for me. It was the first time that someone gave me something just to be generous on my trip, but it wasn't my last. I was soon to find out that many Americans are really generous.

We made it almost to Denver that day. He stopped at a rest area. He slept in the cab and found a place with the cargo for me to sleep in my sleeping bag. The next morning, he dropped me off in Denver.

This day was quite memorable for me. My kids tell me that I am clueless when it comes to women. It probably explains why I was a virgin so long. I wish I hadn't been so clueless that day. I had gotten rides up to near Breckenridge when I decided to stop for breakfast. I had french toast. I didn't drink coffee in those days, so I'm guessing I had orange juice. I was still very clean-cut at that point in my trip. I had only slightly long hair, my jeans didn't have any holes in them, and I had recently had a shower. Anyway, when I went to pay my bill, I had to cash a traveler's check. It was my mom's idea, and it wasn't like I knew how I should be doing this. My mom thought I should have traveler's checks, and so, I got traveler's checks. I know I'm making a big deal about the checks. I'm stalling. Anyway, the cashier and manager were reluctant to cash it, I suppose because I had a backpack. They cashed it, but I don't think I actually knew what the problem was at the time.

The restaurant that served me my breakfast so well was down the frontage road a little way from the on-ramp to the interstate, but it was within walking distance. The morning was cool and crisp. Do you see what I'm doing here? I'm trying to set some kind of mood of the situation by describing the environment, like I've seen better writers do in their books, but I can't seem to do a better job of describing it than, "The morning was cool and crisp." The problem is that I can't seem to find a better way of doing it than that, because that was the best way. I had just come off the prairie in early September, where the weather had been cooking and rose up a couple of thousand feet, which made the air cool and crisp. I apologize for the lack of creative phraseology, but damn it, the air was cool and crisp.

I was walking down the road in new jeans, T-shirt, boots, and a hat. I had bought all new stuff before I left. The jeans hadn't been worn but maybe twice. They were still blue and unfaded, as was my T-shirt, which was either navy blue or dark green. I was so proud of my boots because I thought they looked so different with their waffle pattern on the bottom. The problem was that I was wearing a cheap knock-off of the boots that were popular in the mountains at that time. That wasn't the first time that I had chosen something that was not quite the same as what everyone was wearing at the time. I blame that on my upbringing. My mom was always doing that. We never quite caught on to that "being stylish" thing. We always thought a few dollars off was close enough.

My hat was green. It was similar to those hats golfers wear with a narrow bill that went halfway around the head and some cloth that came up over the top and snapped to the bill. I call them a be-bop hat, but I'm sure that's not the name of them. I always had a thing for hats. I once wore around an old Brownie hat for a couple of weeks that I had cut off a loop on the top and painted black. Everybody kept asking me if I was Jewish. I said no. I also used to have a Frank Sinatra hat—you know, one of those plaid hats that I think they call a fedora. Anyway, my green hat was similar to the golf hats, but as I said, for a few dollars less, you can get something that's close enough.

I must have been quite a sight. There I was, starting off on my big adventure, walking down the road with a beautiful view, and wearing my brand-new clothes and brand-new bag. I might as well have had *virgin* tattooed across my forehead.

Two attractive young girls about my age noticed that I had had some trouble getting my check cashed. As I was walking down that road, they offered me a ride. They brought up the trouble I had had with the check as a conversation starter. Their names were Joan and Karey. When I got in their station wagon, they said they were going to friend's place in Breckenridge and wanted to know if I wanted to come along. I'm thinking I said okay, even though it was contrary to what I had planned. Sometimes I have a hard time getting off a plan.

Maybe I said it earlier, but I can be oblivious to women's intentions. When we got there, I found out that their friend, John, was a guy that was a couple of years older than me. He had long blond hair and wore faded jeans and the real waffle boots that were so popular in the mountains. He was staying in the cabin of a friend of his that was at work that day. This is where I wasn't too bright. I have had 20/20 hindsight quite often in my life. Two girls pick up a guy and take him to a cabin where there was already a guy. Two girls and two guys. Now I know they wanted to make it even. It's hard to explain why I felt so awkward and didn't feel like I could do the common male ritual of coming on to a woman. The worst part of this fiasco was that I thought Karey was very attractive. They had even made some obvious remarks about their open beliefs about sex.

"A lot of our friends don't think we should have our open views toward sex. If we want to screw a guy, we just do it," Joan said. I was across the room, sitting in a recliner. To tell you the truth, her statement probably wasn't that blatant. I just feel like that now.

"Well, let's stop messing around and get down to some serious fucking," I replied. You and I both know that I didn't say that. I was too backward to come straight out and say what I felt. I still have trouble saying what I feel today. I didn't come close to letting Karey know what I felt.

Anyway, to make a long story short, I blew an opportunity to cure the dreaded disease of virginity when it was practically spelled out to me because I couldn't believe that someone wanted to have sex with me. Come to think of it, I've always had a Groucho Marx philosophy when it came to girls. He once said that he didn't want to belong to any club or organization that would accept him as a member. I sort of felt the same way with women. I always wondered what was wrong with the woman who wanted to be with me. I wanted her to make the first move, and I guess she wasn't that open about it to go that far. Maybe if she would have known I was a virgin, she would have taken the steps to show me the joys of sex. Damn, why do girls have to be so hard to learn? I even thought that if I concentrated real hard, she would pick that up telepathically. It's funny how often you can't seem to get what you want because of fear and doubt. I often wonder what kind of changes would have happened in my life if I had made love that afternoon.

The other thing that made that day memorable was the drive we took. We got stoned and drove through the mountains, and I don't know if I had ever seen anything so beautiful at that point in my life. Notice how often I say the word *beautiful*. I ought to get a thesaurus about now. I've got an idea. Why don't I say the mountains were *majestic* and the colors were *vibrant*? That's not bad describing there. When getting stoned was new, the music was so amazing, the sky and clouds were phenomenal, and the colors and views were to die for. I had never seen anything that had matched that drive that day.

We stopped off at some little bump on the road called Fairplay, Colorado. There was a gas station, a café, and maybe a few more establishments. I don't remember where the other three went, but I was going into the café by myself. This place was sort of a stereotype of any image you might have for a café in some valley in the mountains. It was rundown and small with a screen door in the front. It needed some paint and had been doing its job as a café for a number of years. Just as I was about to grab the handle, someone that I couldn't see said, "We don't let your kind in here." I was surprised, but I didn't contest it, and I just walked away. I guess I thought that if somebody didn't want me around, I'd oblige them. When I saw the others, I told them what happened. John said, "Well, let's just see what they say when I go in."

Obviously, they were more confrontational than I was, but I was willing to follow. I'm pretty good at following. When we got back to the café, the door was locked, and even though John knocked, they wouldn't open up. I often wonder what made them so scared. I always thought it was ironic that this all happened in a place called Fairplay. It's not truly ironic, though. Truly ironic would have been if they called the place "Unassuming" or "Open Minded." Yea, that's it. Forget what I said about the town being called Fairplay. The real name of the town was Unassuming, Colorado. Now that is an ironic story.

That evening, Mike, who owned the cabin where we were staying, came home. We had a pleasant enough evening. At one point in the evening, John said that Joan had been all over him earlier. Even though I remember him saying that, I don't know where Karey and I were when that happened. Somewhere along the line, Mike noted that Karey was real standoffish that evening. I felt that my insecurity that day had ruined her day and made her insecure because she wondered what was wrong with her.

The next day, after having bologna and eggs, they took me back to the highway and suggested that I go south toward Aspen, but I decided to go back to the interstate and head west toward California. Remember, I was not yet a truly free spirit. I had plans to go to California, so a trip to Aspen would have really knocked me off of my plans. I definitely had the feeling that they were glad to see me go. I also think that they thought I was gay. John, Joan, and Karey, if you're reading this, I wasn't gay, I was just a virgin. In fact, thinking about hugging and kissing guys gives me the willies. If I woke up a woman tomorrow, I would have to be a lesbian, because I just couldn't be with a guy. I definitely have a thing for that furry patch between a woman's legs. Karey, I wanted you in the worst way. Damn insecurity. Although that wasn't the last time that I failed to impress somebody.

It was a beautiful fall day. The sun was out, and the air was crisp and fresh. (There are those words again. Let's have a little exercise. Everybody put down your books and try to describe Colorado mountains without the words *beautiful, crisp,* or *fresh.* Have fun, and get back to me on how you made out.) As I got just past Vail, I was picked up by a guy in a faded blue Camaro. We smoked a joint, which made the trip through what some people call the most scenic stretch of interstate in the country spectacular. This was part of the adventure that I had been looking for. It was all new to me, which made it exciting. The highway runs along the Eagle River between Eagle and Glenwood Springs, which is a deep canyon with a railroad on the other side of the river. Since then, the government has chosen to spend more money on that stretch of interstate than any other stretch in the country; however, on that day, we were in bumper-to-bumper traffic on one lane. I didn't mind, because I was too busy absorbing everything. I returned and went down that road a few years back. The view is still spectacular, but time has made me less able to get excited about such things. Then again, I wasn't stoned when I took that second trip. I guess there are some good things about being a young, inexperienced man. We were able to enjoy deeper in those days not because they were better times, but because we weren't as jaded.

I was let off in Glenwood still buzzing. The rest of the day was quite enjoyable. I was relaxed and totally absorbed in everything I saw.

When I got to Grand Junction, it was early evening, and I thought I would try an old hustle that I had once heard of. One summer, when my brother was in college, he decided to join a combining crew that worked its way north from Oklahoma to Montana as the wheat ripened. Things went well until they got to Montana, where rain stalled them out for about a week. He had to get back to school, so he cut out and came back before the job was done. He brought a guy named Hoagy with him who had traveled around quite a bit. Don't ask me how he came up with a name like Hoagy, because I don't know. He said that he would often go into a nice restaurant when he was low on cash and ask them if there was something he could do to earn a meal. He said that most of the time, he was given an excellent meal, and he seldom was asked to do anything to earn it. Anyway, I went into a restaurant and was prepared to ask them if there was anything I could do to earn a meal. The strange thing was that nobody came out to ask me what I wanted. Seriously, I must have stood there for at least twenty minutes, and it was as if no one worked there, so I eventually left. Snubbed for the second time in two days! Later that evening, I got a ride with someone who said that a driver had been killed by a hitchhiker a few days earlier. I don't know if it was in the news all over the state, and if that was the reason for the snubbing or not, but it was obvious that a fair number of people in that state did not trust hitchhikers at that time.

As I stood on the on-ramp to the interstate, another hitchhiker, Kevin, who was from England, walked up. We got one or two rides before we called it a day and spent the night in our sleeping bags under the stars in the Utah desert. That ended the third day of my adventure.

CHAPTER 3

Los Angeles

It was cold that night. It wasn't real cold, but Kevin and I were uncomfortable as we waited for a ride the next morning. The strange thing I remember about that morning was Kevin saying as he lit up a cigarette that it felt good to have something warm to suck into his lungs when it was cold. I didn't smoke at the time, but within a couple of months, I would be smoking. Looking back now, I realize that people use a lot of reasons to rationalize smoking. I smoked for five years and then quit. I am constantly around teenagers now and have come to the realization that only teens will pick up a pack of cigarettes, read on the side that it can cause cancer or heart problems, take their puff off of a cigarette and cough their lungs out, but still start smoking because they think they look so good doing it. Smoking gives a nondescript person a chance to express him- or herself so many times in some small way. You can't tell me that Humphrey Bogart or John Wayne didn't use cigarettes as part of their identity. Okay, if the ancient references don't help, think of Bruce Willis trying to be so tough against impossible odds as McCain without cigarettes. That's why I'm such a pussy now: I can't be tough without a cigarette.

The first ride we caught that morning was with a man going all the way to Los Angeles. Mitchell, the driver, had a red Buick that was about five years old at the time. He was headed to Orange County, where his sister lived. There was something about Mitchell that said that he wasn't telling the whole story. He said that he might stay awhile, but he wasn't traveling with a lot of possessions. He got a strange look on his face whenever he talked about his sister. He said he was from Ohio but wouldn't talk much about his life back there. I don't remember hardly anything of the ride itself. I think I slept a good portion of the way.

We spent the evening in Las Vegas. We got a small, cheap room, and Mitchell got some sleep while Kevin and I went out and checked out the town a little bit. I'm sure Mitchell paid for the room because he felt he needed the rest, and I also know that I was too cheap to contribute much.

I was underage, so I couldn't gamble. I'm thinking that Kevin must have been too young too, because he didn't leave me there to go gamble. The only place we could get into was Circus Circus. Circus acts were being performed in the middle of the place, and I guess it was trying to get some family business by allowing underage people in. I don't know if that worked out for them or not. I don't know if the place is still there or not. I do know that Vegas is not real interesting for you if you can't get in anywhere. To this day, I have no real desire to go to Vegas, but I don't believe that comes from my previous experience. I believe that comes from the fact that I have never come out of a casino with more money than I went in with. I have no luck when it comes to gambling, and that's because of the way I drove as a teenager; the fact that I lived through my teenage years means that I used up all my luck. That's not the only reason I haven't won at a casino. It's also because I haven't had to deal with bad things when it comes to my family.

I have led a charmed life when it comes to my kids' and my health. I have been extremely lucky in my life, and since a person can only have so much good luck, I can't have everything. It has led me to believe that my karma will not let me win. If I were to win big at a casino, I would be nervous until enough bad luck had come my way to make up for the good luck. Sometimes I go to a casino and blow some money, as if

I am making a payment to the luck gods so that I won't have real bad luck creep into my regular life. You're probably wondering about a guy that would put that much thought into such a stupid idea. To enjoy gambling, you have to be excited about the possibility of hitting the big one. I've never felt that.

We went back to the motel and left for LA about two in the morning. We got there while it was still pretty early. I knew two people from my hometown who were living around Los Angeles. One was Matt, who I had known since before kindergarten, and who I been best friends with from time to time while we were growing up. Matt was always a good friend. I did not, however, have an address for him, and I had only had a slight notion of how to get in touch with him. The other guy was Brad, who I had hung out with some. Brad was a couple of years older than I was and the older brother of a girl I had been in classes with since I was in fifth grade, but I definitely didn't know him very well; however, I did have an address for him.

I'm sure he had gone to college for two years. I can't tell you what he was thinking when he quit school, packed up everything into his Volkswagen Superbug, and drove practically nonstop to California. He was working in Pomona at a mall selling shoes and was living in an apartment complex in Chino, I think. Why he stopped in that part of the Los Angeles metropolitan area, I'll never know. If you are from those areas, you are probably thinking that that's okay, because you grew up there and your family and friends are there. But if you are from the Midwest, your image of Los Angeles is not Chino or Pomona.

When you pick up from what you know and move to a completely strange place for no real reason, you are taking on an adventure. You are saying that your life needed something new and exciting. Before you take on this adventure, you develop some sort of image of what you think your adventure will be like. I don't know how it is for everybody else, but I mix a lot of daydreams in with any images of my future, which then becomes unrealistic to the point that the event is practically impossible to live up to. I guess nobody dreams up an adventure that is dull and lifeless. I didn't know Brad well enough to know what his image of his adventure was, but I definitely got the impression that his adventure was not living up to his dreams. Somehow, I think that selling shoes and living in a lifeless apartment in a flat piece of desert was not what he imagined. He was also taking on his adventure alone, which makes it harder. I also got the impression that the costs were eating him up, because there wasn't much in the refrigerator, and I don't think he wanted to share much. There aren't many details in my memory to support these feelings, but I didn't feel like he wanted me around. Keep in mind that I may come up with some negative vibes in my own mind due to my own insecurities. But it is easier to believe that he just didn't want me around.

Now, my dream of an adventure was that I was headed to Australia, so I got up one day and made my way into the Australian Embassy. It was not easy to make your way from two-thirds of the way out toward San Bernardino into downtown Los Angeles without a car. There are a million interstates and expressways throughout LA, and it is difficult to hitchhike through that maze. I can't remember one detail of that trip except that my whole plan was shot down. Australia was not letting just anybody in. The exact details of the restrictions are not clear in my memory, but needless to say, you didn't get a visa without money or a skill or both. I suppose I was thinking that I would work my way over on a ship and then just live there. Now I know that that was impractical, but I applaud my young self for making the effort. So there I was in Los Angeles, which is about 1,500 miles from home, with no real plans, but I knew I wasn't ready for my adventure to end.

On the way back from downtown Los Angeles, I took a bus that went east for a long way. It went from a real high-dollar area like downtown LA through East LA and on out into the San Bernardino Valley. I don't know where it ended, but I do know that I made it most of the way back on that one bus.

So that left me with the task of finding Matt. The only address or phone number I had was for someplace in West Covina, which was closer to downtown LA. It took me more than one try, but I finally got in touch with someone who knew where he was and was willing to give me a ride.

Matt was in the environment I wanted to be in. He and his brother were living in a small apartment about three blocks from the corner of Hollywood and Vine. It was a large two-story apartment building that just oozed atmosphere for a couple of yokels from the Midwest. You could walk down the long hallway and hear the people living behind those walls. Everyplace else I had lived in before was a house in the middle of a yard, and you just didn't get the feel of the other people around you.

The apartment had three rooms. The living/bedroom was the first room you saw as you came in the door. The bed was one of those pull-down jobs in a closet that you see in movies. It was convenient, considering the size of the place. Off of that room was a door to the bathroom to the right and an opening to the kitchen on the left. I would venture a guess that the apartment next door was a mirror image of that one. The kitchen had a table and chairs, a sink with a few cabinets, a refrigerator, and a stove. The whole apartment looked like something out of an old detective movie from the forties, which was appropriate for me since we were in Hollywood. The difference in atmosphere between Chino, which is within throwing distance of the desert, and Hollywood is phenomenal.

Matt and his older brother Tim were the sons of a conservative minister for a conservative branch of a common sect of Protestants. Tim was what was called a "Jesus freak." I don't mean that in any negative connotation. He was just passionate about what he believed. He worked for a paper on Hollywood Boulevard called the *Free LA Press* or something like that that was very Christian in all its articles. Matt was the outlaw of his family. He had a knack for getting in trouble in school, although it was nothing serious. It was usually something like getting mouthy with a teacher or just being a disruption in class. I always thought that Matt was better-looking than me, and I was probably right, because he had a very good-looking girlfriend in high school. It is possible, maybe even probable, that he had a good-looking girlfriend because he had more confidence in himself. That's right. I told you about me being backward and insecure about girls, didn't I? He wrestled in high school and was somewhat athletic. About his junior year, he started smoking pot and taking drugs. When I started smoking in my senior year, he and Ken were living in an old farmhouse out in the country, and that was where I first smoked pot. It was common for us to travel down the country roads in his Volkswagen Bug, smoking and jamming to music with friends during that summer after graduation.

I was glad to see Matt. He and I were much more simpatico than Brad and I were. The first or second night I was there, he and I went cruising to see the sights and try to score some drugs. We didn't know anyone, so we didn't quite know how to accomplish this. In my hometown, all the stoners knew each other, so you trusted a guy, or not, based on the dealings you had while you were growing up. Going out and asking complete strangers for drugs was foreign to us. We went to the Whiskey a Go Go and a few other places on Sunset and Hollywood Boulevard and asked around, but we couldn't score anything. Don't you just love how I learned the lingo? The word *score* is a very descriptive word for the activity. When someone does agree to supply you with your particular vice, you feel like you scored. You know, like you made some points in the game of life. I don't know if we didn't look trustworthy or whether we just didn't ask the right people, but no luck. We ended up at a supermarket and bought some cough syrup. We both drank about a bottle and started walking around. Matt threw up what he drank, but I kept mine down and started to feel pretty woozy by the time we decided to go to bed.

The next day, we decided to go to Griffin Park, which I think was within walking distance. Matt felt fine, but I was pretty groggy. I remember looking at some of the plants in the yards around there and thinking that they looked waxy and fake. They were definitely different than what we had back home. I don't remember much else about that day except that I was dragging, but I had a good time because it was so different than anything I had ever seen before.

Since that time, I have been down to the French Quarter, which is one of the biggest freak shows in this country. But at that time, coming from my hometown to the environment of Hollywood and Sunset Boulevards was mind-blowing. I used to sit in one place and watch the freaks walk by. At that time, if you were growing your hair long and getting stoned, you called yourself a "freak" as a term of endearment with the others like you. But I wasn't looking at those freaks; I was looking at strange people doing strange things. I was looking at those freaks as if it were a freak show.

I stayed with Tim and Matt for about three or four days. Since my original plan was destroyed, we talked a lot about what I was going to do. Matt had heard about a place called Laguna Beach where guys lived back in the hills in caves, and it was a happening place. There I go again with the lingo of the times. It almost makes you feel like you're back in the early seventies when I use words like *happening* in that context, doesn't it? I don't believe I came to the decision easily, but I finally decided to hitchhike down there and check it out.

Southern California

When you are from the Midwest, your impression of the southern California coast is determined by television, movies, and magazines. The reality of that day came close to the illusions. I joined up with the Pacific Coast Highway somewhere around Long Beach. The Pacific Coast Highway winds in and around the waterfront as it heads south. Sometimes, the view is interrupted by dunes, hotels, and houses. My first trip driving along the beaches was not disappointing. I imagine that in time, a person can take the views for granted. If you see the same view every day, you no longer see all the beauty that smacks you in the face when you're looking at it for the first time.

The highway sort of wound down from a slight elevation as it approached Laguna. Just as it cleared a hotel on the beach, the beach came up to meet the highway at the end of Laguna Canyon Road before it became surrounded by shops and hotels in downtown Laguna Beach. I write all this in past tense because I haven't been back in thirty-five years, and I don't know if any of it has changed. If some of my recollections are wrong because of the passage of time, I hope you will forgive me.

I got out and spent the afternoon enjoying the beach. Toward evening, I became anxious, because I didn't know how to go about finding this place where people lived in caves. I wasn't sure what to expect. Was it a commune with a lot of people, or was it just a case of going into the hills and finding your own cave? I asked a few people about it, but I didn't get any satisfactory answers. Just about then, a car pulled up to me with a young man and woman in it, and they asked me if I would like to go to a Buddhist meeting. Not wanting to cross off a new experience at that point, I asked them for more information. The girl's name was Jane, and the fact that she was good-looking might have had something to do with my not wanting to blow it off. The guy wasn't good-looking to me, so I didn't give a shit what his name was. She said that I could get anything I wanted by chanting and that they were going up to a house that was up Laguna Canyon Road. I thought that that would get me up into the hills, and I was also curious about how this chanting thing worked, so I said okay.

Oh, yea, did I tell you that she was good-looking? I know some of you know where I'm leading you. I went up to the house and listened to testimonials about how these people had gotten money and things that they needed just by chanting over and over, "Nam myo ho renge kyo." These people could chant this melodically and fast. So I chanted this over and over with a clear desire on my mind. I have no doubt that if I had gotten some pussy that night or in the next couple of days, I would be a Buddhist to this day.

When the meeting broke up, I came to the conclusion that I wasn't going to chant my way into her pants or anyone else's. It was getting late, and I was getting tired, so I asked if anyone knew of this place where people lived in caves. Nobody knew anything about it, but there were caves all up in the hills. I started climbing up into the hills, which were not too steep but were covered with a brush that was dried up and brown-looking at that time of year. I was working my way up a crevice in between two hills and found a small cave just big enough to hold my backpack. I unrolled my sleeping bag and slept out in the open.

The next morning, I got up, put my backpack in the cave, ate a couple of pieces of whole-wheat bread, which I had recently discovered that I liked better than the white bread that I'd grown up on, watched a deer that was about thirty feet away, and then headed down to the highway. Somebody at the Buddhist meeting had told me about a church in Laguna that you could get small jobs through. It was a place where guys would come in and hang around with a ping-pong table and some chairs. People would call in and say they needed some odd jobs done and how much they were willing to pay. The person answering the phone would then go through the list, which was in order of first come, first choice, and see if anyone wanted to take the job.

One time, I took a job paying a dollar an hour doing some odd things around an older woman's house. I say *older* because she was about the age I am now. She was a nice enough woman, and we had some interesting conversations that helped me get my mind straight about what I was doing. When you're in new situations and new environments, it's common to do a lot of talking to different people as you try to get a handle on it. I was full of other people's opinions at that time and was constantly trying to formulate my own opinions. She also fed me lunch. Since I didn't really have any expenses, I got enough to hold me over a few days. I don't remember getting many jobs through that place. Most of them were good for only a day or two and didn't pay much. It was mostly just a place to hang out in the morning, since it closed at noon.

When the church closed about noon, some of the guys that hung out there and I would start roaming down toward the beach. The first time a few of the guys took me down the alley behind a bakery so that we could check out their dumpster, I was a little shocked. I didn't want any of the guys to think that I was too good to do a little dumpster diving, so I went ahead and took some stuff—a lot of it was edible, but stale. After awhile, it was no big deal. I didn't really have to get my food out of a dumpster at that time, because I wasn't broke yet, but I was trying to stretch it out. Besides, I was into the experience of it, remember? Since all these experiences were new to me, I would analyze the fuck out of the lessons I was learning. Later on, I tended to just absorb new experiences without thinking about them much.

Afternoons were spent hanging out on the beach. There's not a lot of describing you can do about hanging out at the beach, because it doesn't differ much. We would sit on some benches in the shade sometimes and sit on some benches in the sun sometimes. Then, to break it up a bit, we would go catch some waves. The ocean felt cold to me, but it wasn't too hard to get used to. Something that was in the water and on the beach that I didn't see in the beach movies was the seaweed. It could get pretty scary to get caught up into a patch of seaweed out in the water. I had never seen such waves breaking on the beach. I had seen the Atlantic Ocean when I was younger, but the waves didn't get as big there as the ones in California. There weren't hardly any waves at the lake back home. If there were even slightly big waves at the lake, then it was too windy to be out on the water. It would have been cool to do some surfing, but I didn't have a board, and it probably would have been impractical for me to purchase one. Even though I probably wouldn't have been very good at it, I think I would have liked doing it.

Hanging out at the job service in the morning was nice and informative. The topics of our conversations were different from what I had known before. This was where I first learned about Mardi Gras. These guys had been leading a life that was different from what I had ever known and was a million miles from anything I had imagined. Reggie was a black guy that hung around there, and he was the first guy that I had ever seen with dreadlocks. He said it came from not brushing his hair as he grew it long. I don't think that's how NFL players today get their hair into dreadlocks, though. Most of the time, I hung out with Ron, Rick, and Georgia.

Georgia had been in and around Laguna for at least four years. He had long hair and a beard and could be considered one of the original hippies. The stories about him were phenomenal. One was that he took about eighty hits of LSD. Another was that for Christmas in about 1968 or '69, the group that Timothy Leary founded when he was making acid in Laguna and promoting acid as a religious experience flew over the beach and dropped thousands of hits of acid with little parachutes and notes telling people to get in touch with their spiritual selves. They said that Georgia was running around, taking handfuls of the stuff. I know enough to know that you can't take old stories as fact. There is a good possibility that those were exaggerated, but I am pretty confident that Georgia took a lot of LSD in his day.

When I met up with Georgia, he was no longer taking drugs. He was into Jesus and the Bible. A lot of people who were heavily into drugs turn to Jesus as a substitute for the dependency they had on drugs. Most of them can't get off drugs without having something major to take its place. Since God and Jesus have very positive associations, it's about the only thing that could possibly fill as huge a hole as the hole left by drugs when major druggies try to get off of them.

Georgia was very upbeat, to the point of being bubbly. He had a great personality, and you had to love the guy; however, when you spent a lot of time around him, you realized that after a half hour or forty-five minutes, his conversation started to come around to same thing. He talked very fast, but he only had about an hour's worth of conversation before he had to repeat himself. I would like to have met him before the drugs took away a big part of his brain. Maybe I'm wrong in assuming that drugs did that to him. Maybe he always had only an hour's worth of views, and it was just different views.

Rick and Ron were who I hung around the most. They had been spending the winters in Laguna and summers in Oregon for years. Rick had a beard and long, reddish-brown hair with blond streaks, and I'm sure he was one of the original hippies. I think he was about twenty-eight or thirty. He was quiet and reserved and never took any of the jobs offered to him. He wore the same clothes every day. His jeans were heavily patched.

In those days, we loved patching our jeans when we got a hole in them. I'm not talking about those iron-on patches that we got when we were little. I'm talking about the patches that we used to have, where you would cut out a piece of cloth that was as big a contrast as you could from the jeans, and then sew them on by hand with a needle and thread.

When the patches got holes in them, you just sewed another patch on top of them. Neil Young's *After the Gold Rush* album cover shows a pair of jeans with patches on them.

Rick had a pair of patched jeans that could have only been acquired with a history. I believe he was on his second or third layer of patches. I don't know how he managed financially, but he lived at the Hotel California, which was where a lot of the guys stayed. I'm pretty sure he could have fallen off the face of the earth and not have more than ten people notice. He was a nice guy, though.

Ron was the guy who formed many of my concepts at that time. One time, after I had been ripped off and was out of money, I said that I was going to call my mom and have her send me some. He told me that I was on my own, and I should make due without calling home every time I needed something. I told him that it was my money that I had saved, and he said that I should just make do with what I had. I was worried about the prospect of running out of money, and he told me that things always come along. At the time, I didn't know what he was saying, but I went along with what he said. Later, I understood what he meant, and I think that philosophy has made things easier on me, even though I've forgotten from time to time.

It is mentally, physically, and emotionally exhausting when you worry about the future. You can't help it! It just creeps up on you. Worrying does nothing to solve the problem, but it's hard to shut it off. Worrying is easier to shut off when you have a feeling and a confidence that things will work out. If we could stop worrying, the world would be a better place. I could get a Nobel Prize if I could just figure out how to stop all the worrying in the world. Hell, the only thing left in the world to solve after that would be world hunger and, of course, how to get more pussy.

Ron also said that Laguna had mellowed out over the years. In the beginning of the Hippie Movement, for the lack of a better phrase, Haight-Ashbury in San Francisco, Berkeley, and Laguna were the happening places to be on the West Coast. Drugs were all over the place, the parties were wild, and the place was crazy. By the time I got there, just a few old hippies like Rick and Ron came back from time to time, and there were some old remnants, like Georgia. Today, people, mostly students, ask me if I was a hippie. When I am answering them in even a slightly serious way, I tell them that I was a later-day hippie, because I was a hippie after it was pioneered. My hippie time was after the time when rednecks would beat the shit out of people who had long hair.

After a couple weeks, I still hadn't come across any pot, and I wanted to get stoned. One evening, while I was trying to make my way back to my cave, a guy going up Laguna Canyon Road picked me up and asked me if I wanted to smoke some pot. Of course, I said yes. He had long, blond hair and looked like a typical California surfer/beach bum. He started driving through some side streets in his Volkswagen and said that his pot was back at his house. He then told me that he was bisexual and his girlfriend was cool with that, and then he wanted to know what I thought of a guy sucking my dick and said since he had long hair, I could pretend it was a chick doing it.

"I realize that out here in California, bisexuality is much more open and accepted," I replied. "However, I am from the Midwest, and we are much more conservative back there, so it's a new idea to me. Even though I'm into gaining experience in my life right now, I think it is just too radical on my feeble Midwestern mindset. I just don't think I can wrap my mind around that yet." Notice how I left it open for the future by saying *yet*. He said that was cool and dropped me off back at the road. I said to myself, *Crap! Who do I have to fuck around here just to get stoned?* Then I realized the answer to that and decided to keep it as it was. I still wanted to get stoned, though.

One night, after I had been there for two or three weeks, a couple of guys came around asking if we wanted some pot, so Ron and I each came up with five dollars, and they wanted me to go with them. (Notice that I stated ten dollars as a price. That's how much it usually was in those days. There was a lot more of it in a bag, too, for that low price. The problem was that it usually wasn't as good as what they have nowadays. The guys growing it now have a lot more knowledge on what it takes to grow the good stuff. It takes a lot less to get you stoned these days.) We walked a few blocks and stopped by a gate. He told me to wait there because the guy he was getting it from didn't want anyone that he didn't know to come in. I said, "Sure, I understand." I didn't want them to think this was my first drug deal I had ever made with a stranger. You've got to appear cool when you're in the middle of a drug deal. Drugs are all about being cool. I waited about fifteen minutes and finally opened the gate. It led to the beach. I'd been ripped off in a drug deal for my first time. How could this be? I had done my best impression of cool.

About a week later, Ron and I each went in half on some pot. He went to get it this time. While I was waiting, a few guys were hanging out by the beach, and someone suggested that we get some Jimson weed. I had never heard of it, and neither had some of the others. The guy that had suggested it said, "Try it; it's good." He then offered to go up into the hills and get some. About a half hour later, he came back. He had some prickly seed pods and started to cut them open. Somebody got some Cokes. He said we were to eat the seeds, but they were very bitter and we would need to drink them down with the Coke. That was an understatement. They were absolutely the most bitterest things that I had ever had. Notice that I thought they were so bitter that I put a double superlative so that you would understand it. That stuff wasn't just most bitter, it was the most bitterest.

We then waited for them to take effect. A couple of us went over to Taco Bell to get something to eat. On our way back, I found it extremely hard to walk. I didn't get back to where we were sitting before I was completely out of it.

Soon, the hallucinations came. Ron and some other guys moved us down the beach behind the hotel. I vaguely remember throwing up, and it's a good thing I did. I don't know how long I went before I came to the part of the evening's festivities that I remember. I was walking back from having a burrito, and the next thing I know, I was fighting aliens on the beach. I talked to people who were not there. I saw an alien spaceship land. There were three aliens. One was about seven feet tall with a backpack that went up over his head, sort of like the way a pickup camper goes over the cab of the truck. By the time you put an over-the-head backpack on a seven-foot alien, that motherfucker was about eight feet tall. He had a nice face, though. Kind. Gentle. Ron said I was eating sand at one point.

At some point, I decided it was time to go to my cave and to bed. I'm not sure why Ron let me wonder off on my own. I walked up to the patio outside the hotel and stopped to take my boot off so that I could knock the ants and snakes off. Before I finished my task and put my boot back on, some asshole wanted to talk to me. I got up to talk to him. During the evening's festivities, I began to realize that some of the people were a hallucination, so after talking for a little while, I began to doubt his reality, and he simply faded out. That bastard distracted me from my boot and then just faded out on me. I think that was rude, to say the least. I never did go back and get my boot. I made it over to Laguna Canyon Road, caught a ride with only one boot on, and climbed up to my cave. The three aliens walked through my campsite while I was putting out my sleeping bag and continued on up the hill. Maybe they were on a mission.

It turns out I also lost my glasses that night. The next day, I put on my Converse tennis shoes, since that was the only pair of shoes I had left. It turns out that I didn't have glasses again for about nine months. That fucking bitter-ass shit made me lose my glasses and one of my boots, two things I didn't need to lose at that point. The topper was that Ron smoked all the pot, and I didn't get any of it.

I had worked the previous day doing some odd jobs cleaning up around someone's house, and I was supposed to come back that day. I made it back and worked that day, but I kept having hallucinations. I just about jumped out of my skin when a stream of water flowing down the street looked like an anaconda out of the corner of my eye. That sucker was eight inches in diameter before I looked at it and saw it wasn't there. Not having glasses helped enhance the hallucinations. Some of the other guys that had eaten the seeds and didn't throw up had hallucinations for days. One guy ended up in jail that night. I never even slightly wanted to go through that high again. I figure that anyone who would do that more than once had to be desperate for a high.

After working for two days and having a little money, I decided to go for a little change in scenery and went down to San Diego for a few days. It was beautiful and sunny that day, but I guess there are a lot of those in Southern California. As I was getting near San Diego, I came upon a guy in his fifties or sixties with long, gray hair wearing a long robe like the kind they wear in the Middle East. He went by J. C., which was short for Jesus Christ. Except for him being older than Jesus got to be, he looked the part. To tell you the truth, he looked more like Charlton Heston playing Moses. He told the guy driving that he used to be a contractor and that he just gave it all up. He said he was going to Ocean Beach. When I said that I didn't know where I was going and that I was just going down to check out what San Diego was like, he suggested I go to Ocean Beach with him.

Ocean Beach looked like it had been a town by itself at one point. Keep in mind that I'm just guessing, but I would guess that San Diego just plain over ran it. It had several blocks of old storefronts that had seen better days, like so many old parts of every city were in those days. I'll bet that it's a lot better nowadays.

When we got there, he led me to a building that used to be a store about a block from the beach that someone rented to have a place for all the transients and bums to hang out. I say *bums* not entirely in a negative way, but to describe the type of person that I was becoming: a person who hitchhikes around, works a little from time to time, takes what's given to him, and does whatever comes to him. There were a lot of us back then. I saw J. C. only a couple of times after that, but everybody knew him, and I could have found him easily if I had wanted to.

When I went down to the beach, they were having some kind of surfing competition. The waves were big that day, probably the biggest I had ever seen before. The beach was nice, and there was a lot of action going on. The beach was on the right and was a typical California beach with plenty of white sand complete with seaweed and anything else that washed up from the ocean. Did you ever notice all the beach movies never showed dirty beaches with all the wood, sticks, and seaweed that drifted up on them? I wonder why that is.

What made this beach different were the rocks off to the left. There was a pretty flat section of rocks that went out about a hundred yards into the ocean. After at least a month of running into very few people offering to sell me any drugs whatsoever, when I went out onto the rocks, it was like a bazaar. It was almost like they had tables and tents set up to sell you whatever you wanted. I have since been to conventions with less merchandise for sale. Of course, I am exaggerating, but I know I ran into four or five guys selling pot and acid out there on the rocks. Within ten minutes, I had scored some pot and some acid. The guy that sold me the acid for two bucks said it was little blue barrels that you could split four ways. Not being very experienced with taking acid, I wasn't totally aware that when people sell you drugs, and especially LSD, they tend to exaggerate the quality of their product. I suppose a lot of them were in training to sell used cars. Needless to say, I didn't really think I could split it four ways. Luckily, I decided to try it out. That evening, I took a third of one and gave a third to someone else. Most acid in those days was either cut with speed or strychnine. This didn't have much of either. It had high acid content. I was up all night hallucinating heavily.

I stayed in San Diego about three days. One morning, right after we had smoked a joint, the guy who sold me the pot, Tom, asked me if I wanted to go get some coffee. Up until then, I hadn't ever really gotten into drinking coffee. My mom and dad always drank their coffee black, and I always thought it tasted nasty. I still do think it tastes nasty black. Anyway, he talked me into drinking some with cream and sugar. He took me to a little coffee shop where the coffee was ten cents and included one refill. We loaded it up with cream and sugar and got a good caffeine rush while stoned. I have drank coffee ever since.

While I was still in San Diego, I got to hanging out with a guy named Craig, who had a dog named Sammy. I always figured that having a dog with you on the road was not really a good thing. There was the advantage of always having a companion, and sometimes people are more generous to a person that has a dog, but it didn't seem fair to the dog when you weren't always sure where your next meal was coming from. Anyway, Craig decided that we should become traveling companions for a while. Something about Craig gave me an uneasy feeling. So the morning that we were taking off, he had to go do something but wanted me to stick around. I took off without him. A couple of weeks later, I was down there and ran into someone I knew, and he said Craig was real mad at me for leaving without him, but I'm glad I did. It usually pays to listen to your feelings about a person. Your subconscious seems to be able to pick up things your conscious doesn't.

When I got back to Laguna, I moved into a cave closer to town that some other guys were living in. It was bigger, and we could actually sleep in the cave out of the weather. About a week into living in the new cave, somebody got into it and ransacked everything. I had some silver dollars stashed in different compartments of my backpack, and they got those. It really pissed me off that somebody decided that they deserved what I had more than I did. Talk about communication problems: when I told my dad on the phone that I had been ripped off, he wanted to know if my backpack was on my back when it was stolen. It wasn't.

One day, somebody told me about Manpower, a company that specialized in temporary work in Santa Ana. Since I was planning to go back to Hollywood, I didn't want to go without any money. I wasn't really making any money from the church. So I hitchhiked to Santa Ana and found the place. They told me they had a job for that evening. I then spent the day hanging out with a Mexican guy named Julio and some other guy that I don't remember much. Julio was the first Mexican guy that I spent any time with. He looked the part of any Mexican living in Southern California with a name like Julio. He looked and talked just like the Mexicans in the movies; however, he broke all my preconceptions about Mexicans. He was a nice guy. Maybe I had some bad preconceptions, but this guy was just like everybody else. You can see how my Midwestern upbringing had not taught me even the basics of what people of other races and cultures were like. That evening, we spent our time loading a boxcar with toilet paper.

The next day, I saw the most amazing carved piece I'd ever seen in my life. I was walking around downtown and decided to go into a museum of some sort. There, I saw an entire Chinese village complete with houses, carts, animals, and people, yet it was carved into a piece of ivory small enough to sit in my hands. I wondered how anybody could have the patience to do that on anything so small and on something so hard to work with. How many hours had that guy spent on it? Since I had recently started doing some carving, I was amazed. All I had been able to carve was some thumbs. I had been proud of what I had produced until I saw that.

I spent the second night in Santa Ana at a Salvation Army. I don't know how I found out about the place, but it was my first time at a Salvation Army. They opened around five in the evening. I arrived early, and so had four other people. I was the youngest one there. Two of the guys were in their late twenties or thirties, and the other two were in their forties. One guy was from Arkansas, which made him stand out because of the stereotyped image he evoked and for something he said when we went to bed. One of the guys in his forties had a lot of personality, and I remember him saying how much he loved the word *balling* rather than fucking. He said it was one of the great contributions of the younger generation.

The first thing you do once they let you in is have a service to praise God and Jesus. After that, you get a basic meal. It's not fancy but usually quite edible. For people who have been on the road and haven't had a good meal for a while, it is lifesaving.

After the meal, everyone takes a shower. I dropped the soap in the shower and bent over to pick it up, and considering all the times I picked up soap during gym and after practice in school, I didn't think anything of it. The other guys made sure to let the young guy know that that was not a "good idea." I took that as good advice, and I'm glad I didn't find out the "hard" way, if you will excuse the play on words.

After the shower, you get an hour or two of watching TV. Finally, everyone sleeps in a dormitory type of room on clean sheets, which can be a wonderful feeling if it's been a long time since you've slept in a bed. That night, we were lying there in bed shooting the shit, as the expression goes. There was only one thing said that night that I still remember, and I will never, ever forget what the guy from Arkansas said. I don't remember what led up to what he said, and I don't think he was joking, but he said that sheep were the next best thing to a woman. I would think that you would have to have tried both to be able to make a comparative statement like that. In fact, the way it was stated, I would think you would have to have experienced a wider variety than just those two choices. Since I was into getting experience at that point in my life, I'm thinking that I should have gone ahead and got me some sheep pussy. I suppose that I just didn't want my first piece of pussy to be from a sheep.

Writing this has made me remember what a great group the Salvation Army is. They are fighting a noble battle in a losing war. Most of you won't understand what I'm saying unless you have been in the same position.

Maybe it was my stay at the Salvation Army or something else while I was in Santa Ana, but I had a bit of an epiphany. I remember thinking that something my parents used to say was so true. I don't really remember what this piece of wisdom was, but I was impressed that they knew it. So often, the things your parents tell you sort of goes in one ear and out the other, and you don't really understand. But there comes a time when you are out on your own that it comes back to you. I found it astounding to figure out that my parents knew some shit. With that, I hope that some of the things that I tell teenagers will someday make a difference.

It wasn't long after I got back to Laguna that I decided to go back to Hollywood. So I left Laguna, which was a big educational experience for me, and I haven't been back since.

One of the things I picked up while I was staying in Laguna was the nasty habit of smoking. Since I have quit and live in a house with two smokers, I have a very negative view of the vice. I believe I tried it one time and realized that it didn't cause a coughing fit since I had already broken in my lungs with marijuana. After that, I'm sure I had some good rationalizations. I remember thinking at one point that smoking helped take the edge off of hunger, but a stronger reason was that I was a teenager. If a person gets to the age of twenty without smoking, then that person stands about a 95 percent chance of never starting. Only a teenager looks at a warning label on a pack of cigarettes and blows it off, knowing that it won't affect him or her; and besides, they look so cool doing it. Hey, I'm beginning to repeat myself. Maybe I've taken too much acid. Oh, no, I remember: I'm getting old and senile.

When I got back to Tim and Matt's apartment, Matt was in Pomona working and staying with friends. Tim let me hang out for a couple of days until Matt got back that weekend. Tim didn't say anything, but I'm not sure that he liked having me around. I sort of passed my time reading, trying my hand at cooking, and taking walks on Hollywood Boulevard. One night, I was walking down Hollywood when some guy pulled over and asked me if I wanted to go have a drink with him. I said okay. All right, so I was very naïve. I had no idea what he was up to. So we got to his apartment, and he fixed me a drink. We talked for a while, and he asked me if I wanted to spend the night. I said okay. All right, so I wasn't naïve; I was stupid. Before long, he let me know what he had in mind. What surprises me even now is that it took me so long to assert myself enough to get the fuck out of there.

One time, I told somebody about the situation, and the guy I was talking to asked me if I "rolled him." He said he would have taken a lamp and smashed it over the guy's head and taken everything he could get his hands on. There was a certain segment of the society that I associated with that enjoyed "rolling faggots." I blame that episode on my Midwest upbringing. In my hometown, if people had inclinations toward being gay, they kept them in the closet. That has to be the reason, because the only other possibility is that I was a fucking idiot. No, it was my upbringing.

On Friday, Matt came back. I told him that I had scored some acid in San Diego. I had been holding onto it all this time. We decided to go to this place, a bar near UCLA that Matt had heard about. We made our way down to Sunset Boulevard and started hitchhiking west. The first car that picked us up was a guy, Stanley, and two girls, Janice and Robin. When we told them where we were headed, they said that they would give us a ride there if we were willing to go with them to the bus station for a little while. We said okay. While we were waiting on them at the bus station, we decided to go in the bathroom and take the acid. We each took about two-thirds of a hit that was supposed to be split four ways.

After a little while, Stanley offered to take us where we were going and leave the girls at the bus station until he came back for them. When we got into the car, we were just beginning to feel the effects of the acid. Then the guy asked us if we wanted to smoke a joint. I'm not sure I remember what we said, but I'm thinking we said yes. When we smoked the joint, everything just exploded. Matt was too fucked up to find the place, so we had him let us off somewhere on Sunset. We were too fucked up to talk at that point.

We sat on the curb in some residential section for I don't know how long smoking cigarettes, talking, and waiting on a ride. I'm amazed nobody investigated why we were there. We couldn't even hold a conversation. Every time we started a sentence, our minds were going too fast to finish it. I do remember we were talking about the little things in life that give you a sense of security, like cigarettes. I do remember that some of the sentences I forgot to finish were finished later when that thought came back by.

Eventually, a car came along and offered us a ride. It was an old car, like from the forties or maybe even the thirties. Remember, I was too fucked up to know. The interior was in beautiful shape. I'm surprised that I noticed that. The driver was in the front, and there was another guy in the back playing with a mouth harp. The sound of that mouth harp in the back was really fucking with my mind. Quite often when you're all fucked up on acid, you imagine sounds around you that aren't always there. So to be sitting in the front and hearing a mouth harp, which is a strange-sounding instrument, behind you when you're not really sure if you're even really hearing it can fuck with your head. Matt said that he thought they were gay. I was too fucked up to tell, but then again, I had already proven that I was unable to spot them. They took us near Santa Monica Beach because all we had to do was walk down the hill to the beach. I think I saw that hill in an old detective movie one time.

We had planned on spending the night on the beach at the State Park of the Pacific in Santa Monica, but it was closed at night. We started to walk south when a guy in a '58 Buick with a Great Dane taking up the whole backseat picked us up. We both sat up front. He gave us a ride south all the way to Newport Beach on the Pacific Coast Highway. We stopped and had coffee at a little old diner along the way.

By that time, we were coming down and wanted a place to crash. It was about three or four in the morning. The guy driving suggested that we go to a huge apartment complex and jump the fence to the pool, so we did. We went skinny-dipping and then slept a couple of hours. We got up early because we didn't want to get caught in the pool area. Considering the circumstances, our little trip could have turned into a disaster. I felt like I had had a good time. I liked having a really strange experience with an old, good friend.

Some people have what I call a "mental flexibility." You know how you wake up in the morning after having done a lot of physical activity the day before and your body is all stiff and you need to stretch just to be able to walk? That's what living at home in a small town can be like when it comes to your mind. You think that the routine of your life has to be a certain way, and it takes a good stretching to get you moving forward. That mental stretching involves a series of activities that are extremely contrary to your normal movement. You have to be put into a position that is opposed to the way you're accustomed.

Once your body gets flexed and stretched, it can then go to its extremes. Only by pushing your body to its extreme can it grow to new possibilities. Likewise, you must stretch your mind to extremes so that it can grow to new possibilities. By doing this often, you develop a mental flexibility that enables you to respond to circumstances that are not normal. This trip was developing into a situation that required us to roll with the punches. The circumstances of the past month were enabling me to cope with life's oddities. Or maybe it was just because I was young.

As we were walking out of the area, a guy in a Volkswagen van pulled up and asked us if we wanted a ride. We said sure and that we were trying to find the Pacific Coast Highway. He said he was going to San Diego and wanted to know if we wanted to go along. I don't know that Matt was eager, but he said okay. The guy in the van was a surfer, and he wanted to check out the waves at a few of the beaches on the way. We eventually made it to San Diego, and since the only place I knew was Ocean Beach, I asked to be dropped off there. I saw a few guys that I had met when I was there before. It was nice of them to admit they knew me.

We spent the night there and headed back to Los Angeles the next day. It took us all day to make it back to his apartment. On the way back, Matt said that the trip had convinced him that he wanted to get off drugs for a while. It would be hard for me to believe that everybody who does drugs doesn't get those thoughts from time to time. Sometimes, it feels like it's getting to be too much to deal with. I guess if there is somebody who doesn't have those thoughts, it's those poor lost souls that have to spend every minute of every day stoned or drunk. I saw him about a year later back home, and he said that idea didn't stick. As soon as somebody said, "Hey! Let's get stoned," it was lost.

I felt my adventure wasn't over. I still wanted to see something different, so sometime that week, I started north along the PCH. I was ready to be a full-time bum. Maybe I wasn't really ready to be a bum, because I still didn't know what it was like to be hungry with no money and no immediate prospects. Right now, I don't think I understand why I decided to do this. I guess I knew I was in the process of getting an education. I knew there were more ways of getting an education than just by going to school. That wasn't it. I could have gotten an education in a number of ways besides hitchhiking around the country. It wasn't just the hitchhiking. For some reason, I had decided that being a bum was the best way to go. Get Real. The real reason was because I couldn't go back. Can you imagine how it would have been to go back home and say I changed my mind, that I didn't want to be out there? Being a bum at that time was preferable to going back home and telling everybody that I had changed my mind. Stubbornness wins again.

CHAPTER 5

Phoenix by Way of Northern California and Salt Lake City

You would think that I would remember a lot about my trip north along some of the prettiest country known, but the only part I remember was Big Sur. I believe I must have gone a ways on I-5 before I cut over to the Pacific Coast Highway. I think I bypassed Santa Barbara and Ventura. I'm disappointed that I don't remember much, because I haven't had a chance to go that way again since that day more than thirty-five years ago, and I don't believe I'll be out that way again for a while. I'm sort of wondering now how it didn't leave an impression on me. After all, it was all still pretty new to me.

It took me all day to get up to Big Sur. The sun was just going down over the ocean, and the sky was so full of color with just enough clouds to add texture and serenity to the picture. Up ahead, I could see the road rising up along the rock cliff that just came straight out of the ocean. There was a point stretching out into the water that was so well defined, and I could see the road curve at the top of the point back inland and out of sight. I know you are probably tired of hearing me say this by now, but it wasn't the kind of sight you saw back in the Midwest. Now, I don't really want to say it, and you definitely don't want me to say it, but it really has to be said, because talking about a wonderful view requires me to say it. It looked pretty enough to be on a postcard.

I was dropped off in the community of Big Sur. I want to say it was a romantic or sleepy little village nestled in the forest, but I don't know if that's a good phrase for it. It certainly was a unique and picturesque village. Either way, I don't think words describe some places very well, and I don't remember enough details to do the place justice.

It was dark, and I needed to go to sleep. I walked away from the highway into the woods a few yards, found a cozy little place between some trees, rolled out my sleeping bag, and settled in for the night. Soon, I started to hear some dogs barking, and they wouldn't stop. After a while, I heard them running around in the woods around me, and then they found me. It was too late by then for me to get up and go, but finally, a guy shined a flashlight in my face and asked me what I was doing. I never did get a look at his face. What do you say to someone in a situation like that? Oh, yea, you probably wouldn't be in a situation like that. Anyway, I told him I was just crashing for the night. We used to say that back then. We didn't go to sleep; we crashed. At that time, he replied, "Make sure you pick up all your trash when you leave in the morning." Then he left me alone. I wonder if he still remembers the time he found a complete stranger sleeping in his yard. Maybe it happened to him a lot back in those days. I'll bet it hasn't happened to him lately. If you're reading this right now, fellow, thanks for letting me camp out in your yard.

The next day, I made it to Berkeley, the happening place of the late sixties. While I was walking around, some guy asked me if I wanted any drugs. I asked him if he had any acid. He said he did and gave me a pill that looked like a Pepto-Bismol tablet or something out of a drugstore for two dollars. Two dollars was the usual price for acid. I took it and waited for something to happen.

As I said earlier, acid is some dangerous shit. In the beginning, a lot of acid takers try to put themselves in a place where they won't freak out or end up jumping off a building thinking they can fly. That sort of takes planning, and it requires being around someone that you trust; however, with just about all things, we start thinking we can relax those rules because, after all, we know what we're doing. As soon as someone says they know what they're doing, you should run away—or at least duck. It is inevitable when you deal with drugs that you either get more involved with the drugs or you stop. If you stop, then you don't let the drugs get the best of you, but if you like the drug and decide you would like to do it again, then you come one step closer to, in the terminology of our present youth, becoming its bitch. There would be no addictions if that first time was always a horror story. Once you start making love to that drug on a regular basis, it starts working its tentacles into your soul. It becomes the norm, and you feel like there is a hole in your life without it.

I say all this because I was beginning to relax some of my rules concerning acid. Being on the streets of Berkeley was not a safe environment, and that asshole selling me the acid was not someone I should have trusted.

I waited for a half hour, and nothing happened. I saw him and told him nothing was happening, and he said something like, "It will. It's just slow to kick off." So I waited awhile longer, and still, nothing happened. I was beginning to suspect that it was indeed Pepto-Bismol. The good news was that my stomach felt fine. He was still hanging around, and I figured surely, he wouldn't rip me off and then just hang around. I guess he figured that I wasn't going to have the guts to do anything about it. He was right. I didn't confront him. Maybe he figured that I wouldn't kick his ass for two dollars. Maybe he just didn't care whether I kicked his ass or not. Later, I bought some acid from somebody else. It at least had some acid in it, but it was very weak.

I guess that's the sign that a place is over the hill, when you're talking about "happening" places. If the drugs are weak because somebody is cutting it down so much so that they can make a little more profit, then we are talking about the breakdown of that society. I keep wondering how the generation that was supposed to have these high ideals like peace and love could produce corporations that are trying to cut everybody's throats, like the banks nowadays are doing. I'll bet some of the executives at Bank of America started out cutting their acid down to the point that the average hippie couldn't even get a buzz. I'll bet the banks now are using drugs as a sort of minor league training to be an officer at the bank. They're probably scouring the drug cartels right now for their next vice president. There's only one name I could call them, and that would be "rat bastards."

I stayed in Berkeley about two days and then left. I didn't really like it. I felt like the place was burnt out. Probably, two guys ripping me off had something to do with it. I crossed over into San Francisco via the Oakland Bridge that collapsed in the earthquake in '89. I spent the night in San Fran and then went north by way of the Golden Gate Bridge. I wish I had spent a little more time in San Francisco. It's just wrong when a young man who is in training to be a hippie just blows right by Haight-Ashbury and the rest of San Francisco.

The Coast Highway north of San Francisco is quite picturesque. The road winds along a rocky coast. I have just a few memories of stretches of that highway, but I remember more my impression of that area. I believe that I would probably rather live in Northern California than Southern, as far as beauty. I do remember a young guy picking me up in a van with a lot of other people. He got a flat outside of Eureka. When I was in high school, if someone got a flat, we did a sort of fire drill to see if we could set a new record for getting it changed the fastest. When I started doing that with his van, he got quite upset, because he was afraid it was going to fall off the jack. It was a valid concern, considering those were the jacks that hooked onto your bumper and jacked the back end up real high to get the wheel off the ground. When they let me off in Eureka, I think they were glad to see me go. I guess we've all been in a situation where you just rub everyone the wrong way—or maybe it's just me.

I spent the night in Eureka at a Salvation Army. I think I was one of only two people there that night. I had finally reached that point that I had been dreading. I was flat, dead broke. Ron told me that things would work out, and that something always comes around. I wanted to test that theory out, but I kept thinking, *What if something doesn't come around?* I would soon find out. Believe it or not, this time produced a significant part of what I am today. Having ten cents in your pocket with no outlook on where your next meal is coming from changes you. Tough times change people in different ways. Some people might take the Scarlet O'Hara approach and say they will never go hungry again no matter what they have to do. Others learn a confidence in the fact that you will get through this and better times will come. Quite often, it comes in the form of a person who cares about others.

The next day, I went east to Redding. I guess the excitement of the adventure was wearing off, because I know that that is some phenomenal country up there, but I don't remember any specifics. Maybe that was because the weather wasn't the kind of weather that made you fell all warm and bubbly. Isn't it funny how all your good memories involve lovely weather. There was a large change in altitude. Add to that that it was November, and the weather was not totally comfortable. The next day, it rained, so I was just hanging out in the bus station and beginning to feel hungry. Along comes Tony. He walked up and asked, "How long have you been out on the road? Are you hungry?"

It turned out Tony had been out bumming it for a year. He took me off to get breakfast, gave me what cash he had on him at the time, and gave me his old sleeping bag which was a lot better than mine. He had just come back to his hometown because someone he knew died and he was going to inherit some money. I don't think it was a lot. He spread some stories about Mardi Gras and Key West and reaffirmed what Ron had said about something always comes along. I spent the morning with him, but he said he needed to get back because he had some stuff to do. He was definitely one of the good stories of my trip.

The next day I headed south toward Sacramento and then went east toward Reno and Salt Lake City. It had just gotten dark and rainy when I got to Reno. I was in the last ten pages of a novel so I ducked into the bathroom of a service station so that I could be dry while I finished the book. I think it was <u>The Other</u>. I think the gas station attendant thought I was crazy sitting in the bathroom on a rainy night reading a book.

I was doing a lot of reading since I started on my trip. I had probably read ten to fifteen books since August. Matt had told me of some books by a university researcher by the name of Carlos Castaneda. He wrote some books about a medicine man for the Yaqui Indians who used Jimson weed as one of his methods of finding truth or maybe power. Anyway I read a couple of those books. I also read a few of the Chronicles of Narnia. I also read some trash. I had a lot of time to kill. It wasn't all adventure.

When I got to Salt Lake City, I wasn't feeling too good. I had a bit of fever. I spent the nights camping out behind some bushes next to a church. I had discovered that whenever I needed a place to sleep that nobody would bother me if I hid out by a church. During the day, I just hung out at the bus station. It was dry and warm, and nobody bothered me. I heard that a storm was coming, so I decided that I should head south so I headed for Phoenix.

By evening, the storm had caught up with me. I was out on a lonely country road, no rides were coming by, and it was cold. I climbed under a bridge, put all the warm clothes on that I had, and crawled into my sleeping bag. It's a good thing I got a better sleeping bag from Tony, because I froze my ass off as it was. I shivered all night. When the sun came up, I packed up and got out to the road. It was cold as hell and so hard getting out of the sleeping bag. I was miserable out on the road that morning.

It wasn't long before a young guy with an old car picked me up. He didn't take me far, but he dropped me of at a café and asked me if I had any money. I said no, and he gave me two dollars and apologized that it wasn't more. Back then, two dollars could buy a pretty good breakfast. Those two dollars bought maybe the best damn breakfast I have ever had. Contentment is a relative and momentary thing usually, but after having been so miserable earlier, I felt pretty content after that breakfast.

I was hitting Northern Arizona toward evening of the next day. I hadn't had anything to eat since breakfast the day before. It was the longest I had ever gone without eating, and I might have had fifteen cents in my pocket. The thing about riding through Utah and Northern Arizona is that you may hit long stretches of highway that look the same and are of no special value to you. Then you round a corner and see a sight that is fantastic. There was one time that as the road was clinging to the side of a hill, and as we rounded the corner, I saw a gigantic silver bridge spanning a canyon that was fantastic. It's funny what sticks in your memory and what doesn't.

I was picked up south of Winslow by two guys going to Phoenix. The driver was tall and had short hair. The other guy had longer hair and was also tall, but not as tall as the driver. They had some bread and bologna in the back and told me I should fix a sandwich. I was not usually a fan of bologna, but that sandwich was good. It felt good looking out the side window toward the west, eating that sandwich and getting my first look at a desert sunset. Desert sunsets usually have no clouds in sight with a thick yellow-and-orange band across the horizon. The colors are very intense, and then they just melt into the deep blue of the sky.

When we got to Phoenix, the driver put me up in a Holiday Inn in Scottsdale for the night and gave me what change he had. That guy was a truly good person. Once I got settled in my room, the desk clerk brought up a cheeseburger from the kitchen and gave me a couple of dollars. She made me promise to call my mom every so often and let her know how I was doing. I told her I kept in touch every week. I was telling the truth about that. When she dropped me off at the interstate, my mom insisted that I call or write to her every week, which I had done. It turned out that the desk clerk had a son that ran away from home, and she hadn't heard from him since. That must have been difficult for her. Being generous to me did not solve her problems and pain, but sometimes all you can do is try to do what's right and hope that things will turn out okay.

C H A P T E R   6

Phoenix

It was getting along toward the middle of November. I had heard from somebody that Tempe was the best place around Phoenix that a guy like me should go. By that, I mean a bum, a hippie, a freak, or a free spirit, whichever term you would like to use best. I made my way down Van Buren Street, which is an old part of town. In the early '70s, most of Phoenix was relatively new. Phoenix had grown a lot in the previous twenty years. So when I say it was an old part of town, I mean it was the old and depressing part of town. Finally, Van Buren crossed over an old, wide, dried-up (at least, it was at that time of year) riverbed, which put you into the old section of Tempe and not far from Arizona State University.

Just before you got to the bridge across the river, there was a roadside park with a lot of open space behind it. It was sort of a piece of wild, untouched Arizona in between Tempe and Phoenix. I suppose it's all filled in with buildings by now. Looking at a map of the area now, I think it might be covered by an interstate. Anyway, that little park is where I spent the next two or three weeks.

In the front of the park were two shelters with picnic tables and benches. In all the time I was there, we never had any authority figures, such as police officers, come and check things out to decide whether we belonged there or not. I find it amazing that nobody decided that they needed to clean all the vagrants and bums out of that area.

For the first few days, there were four of us. There were actually more than four of us, but I hung out with just four of them, for the most part. Richard was older, had a motorcycle, and was on his version of an adventure. Dave and Bobby were younger and had nothing, just like me. They were runaways. Things were not good for them at home, and, in their opinion, sleeping on a picnic table in a rest area was better than being at home. I think Bobby was only sixteen. He didn't talk about home much, but I'm guessing it couldn't have been good, because, otherwise, why would you want to be out on the road rather that be at home doing what other sixteen-year-olds were doing? Bobby stayed for almost two weeks before he decided that home was not that bad.

Richard only hung around a couple of weeks before he decided to point his motorcycle east. He had come from Northern California, and in the process of heading south, he came through that section of Nevada that is famous for their legal activities with women. In case you didn't catch on, he went to a whorehouse in Nevada. When he went in, they had all the available girls line up so that he could decide which one he wanted. He said they all looked good, so he couldn't decide. He then proceeded to move forward as he was trying to decide, and they started pulling him back and telling him to please decide. Eventually, he picked one and took her to bed. Now that I read this, it's not that good of a story. Most of you that have actually gone to a whorehouse probably have a better story. This is definitely one of those stories that you can say, "I guess you would have had to have been there." A lot of the stories I tell are like that, though. This story was a lot better when Richard told it.

The guy I spent most of my time in Phoenix with was Dan. Dan was from Denver. He was more like me, trying to get out and see the world. He was living with his sister and brother-in-law in Denver after his mother died, which I believe was when he was fourteen. I don't know if I ever knew the whole story as to why he took off for the road. He got along okay with his brother-in-law, but I would imagine that it would be difficult for a young couple to take on a teenager. No matter how noble your ideas were when you took it on, after a while, little things would start to mount up and overtake you. Of course, the intentions are not always so noble. I can personally testify that Dan was not perfect and was capable of being a pain in the ass. He was also a bit on the stubborn side. A lot of people are stunned when I say this, but teenagers are difficult to deal with for people who are quite sure of themselves and damn near impossible for someone that is having trouble keeping his or her own shit together. So to make a short story long, Dan probably decided that it was time that he got out on his own, and they said just what a teenager didn't want to hear, like, "Clean your room," so he up and split.

We were in the process of learning the lessons of the road together. We spent a majority of our time finding something to eat. There was a mission down in the wino section of Phoenix not far from Van Buren that served lunch every day about noon. A good-sized crowd would start gathering about a half hour before they opened up. Phoenix had a large population of winos at that time of the year, being as it was far enough south for people not to have to suffer a harsh winter. At least in Phoenix, when you passed out at night in December or January, you didn't freeze to death. When they opened the doors at whatever appointed time it was, everyone would push as hard as they could to get in early. It was chaos. I saw many a delicate wino go down hard in that crowd. I suppose they survived. Winos can be tough little buggers at times. Everyone wanted to get in early, because this place got most of its food donated from establishments where they considered the food too old to sell to customers but not too old for winos. The better food went to the first to arrive. The further back in line you were, the worse the food got. I have to say this: winos are not a picky lot. They'll eat anything if it's free, so that they don't have to waste good wine money on food. I don't really want to knock the food at St. Vincent's, because they did the best they could with what they got. It sustained us. At times, though, I believe that some of the food had gone south. If you couldn't eat the doughnut, then it did pretty good as a weapon.

The rest of our time, we went into Tempe out in front of a supermarket and panhandled for spare change. Forgetting my dignity and asking a total stranger to give me their spare change for the first time was very, very difficult for me. It didn't take long for that to wear off. When you see someone give you a hateful look—or maybe even worse yet, when they walk right by and pretend to not see you rather than look you in the eye—it makes you feel bad. I know what you're thinking. You are thinking, *Ah, that's a shame!* and I agree with you; however, every time someone does give you something, it makes it easier to ask the next person. Every panhandler has heard how beggars in cities like New York would make thirty or forty dollars a day. That's not much now, but it was a living back then.

I suppose there were people that made a living off of asking others for their spare change, but I couldn't imagine how a person like that could have an ounce of respect for him or herself. Many people realize that there are a lot of winos that are always asking for money, not because they need food, which they do, but because they are looking for enough for another drink; therefore, the "beggees" don't mind coming out of the store with some chicken or sandwich stuff just in case the "beggars" really are hungry, but they will not give you their change. In our case, that was okay, because we really were hungry. Winos are the reason that a lot of people make comment that every panhandler has heard a bunch of times, "Why don't you get a job? I did." You may have noticed that I have not written kindly of winos. There is a good reason for that, though. The reason is that most winos have no real value. They consume more than they produce. Most of them will not be remembered by anyone and will be a net loss on the books of society. I know what you are thinking. You think I'm worried about the low sales of my book in the wino sector, but I figure the rat bastards don't read books anyway. I don't have to worry about them kicking my ass, either, because you can always distract them with a couple of quarters thrown on the ground while you make your getaway.

Some of the time, I got to hanging out with Tommy. It was hard to tell how much of what Tommy said was true. You know how sometimes a person tells you so much that you don't know what is true and what is not? Nothing he or she tells you is unbelievable by itself, but over the long haul, you begin to think that not everything is true. But of course, you don't want to call him a liar. However, I have also been told that I was full of bullshit, even though I know for a fact that my stories were true.

Well, anyway, that was Tommy. No one thing made me think he was lying, but some of it didn't quite match up. He said he was a junkie, even though he hadn't done any recently. He used the phrase "locked up," which I didn't immediately understand. He said that he had taken second in state in wrestling one year in Virginia because he was getting locked up when he wrestled. He said that Johnny Winters was a junkie and that when he was playing his best, it was because he was locked up. After a while, I got to thinking that when junkies haven't had a fix in a while, their skin gets to crawling, and their whole body gets to jumping; they are getting locked up.

Now, I've never been a junkie, so I wouldn't know whether that's an accurate description of what it's like. In fact, since I haven't experienced it, then my description has to be wrong. He told me that one time, after a cop had handcuffed him, he proceeded to beat the piss out of the cop, even though the cop was about six-foot-two and about 220 pounds— and Tommy had handcuffs on. Part of the reason I never crossed him off as a liar was because there seemed to be a tragic streak hiding under the surface. It's hard to put my finger on it, but I felt like that at any moment, he might go crazy and do just about anything, and it didn't seem like it would be positive. As a matter of fact, I heard from somebody later that he had gone crazy one day, stolen a car, got into a high-speed chase with the cops, crashed the car, and then proceeded to fight it out with them. If that was true, that might qualify me as a prophet.

After my meal at the mission on Thanksgiving, I got sick as a dog. I trotted to the restroom often. I also got what I call a sour stomach for the first time. I have had it several times since then. Every time I have gotten it, it was after eating something that has been left out too long or too much. I believe I had food poisoning.

This all happened right after I had my backpack and everything in it stolen. The park had a big open area behind the shelters, away from the highway. I don't believe I ever made it all the way to the back of the park. It was like a little wilderness there in the city. All the way back was a huge rock that could be classified as a hill by itself. It had to be thirty feet high and a couple hundred feet long. I don't know how wide it was, because I never went that far back. Anyway, Dan and I got to sleeping back away from the highway under some trees. We decided to just hide our stuff back in the weeds during the day when we were out begging or doing stuff. It's funny; for almost two weeks, we left our packs under one of the shelters, in plain sight, and never had anything stolen. However, on about the second night that we decided to stash our stuff out in the open space behind the park, we got ripped off. Probably a junkie stole our stuff. They don't care about anybody or anything except their next fix.

I was probably the worst off I had ever been at that time. I rode with Richard on his motorcycle over to the employment office to maybe get a little work. After all, I needed to get all new stuff, because they hadn't just rifled through it like they did in the cave in Laguna; they took everything. I had spent the entire night shivering with just a blanket I had gotten from someone. Richard needed to work some because he had a motorcycle to feed. When we got to the place, I couldn't go anywhere too far from a bathroom, and I think I fell asleep in the waiting room. Nope, I didn't work that day.

Finally, after I started feeling somewhat better, Dan and I went to Manpower and got a job at a Holiday Inn renovating one wing. Things started out good. The guy in charge of maintenance was in charge of the remodeling. First day, he set up a room that we could go to when we finished what we were doing so that he would know where to find us and so that we wouldn't be out in the open. Glen was a good enough sort. He was forty-five to fifty years old and had been a prisoner of war to the Germans during World War II. The guy that managed the hotel was a

German that was a prisoner of war to the Americans. That was an odd coincidence. He was also an ex-smoker. Nobody hates seeing someone smoke worse that an ex-smoker.

Most of the time, all we did was move everything out of the rooms, but we did just about anything that they needed done while they redid the rooms completely. There was also a girl and a guy working with us who worked for the hotel full-time.

After a little more than a week, Dan decided he had had enough with Arizona and wanted to see the West Coast. He went on his way, and I went back to the Holiday Inn. So I was sitting in the room that Glen had set up for us when he came steaming in and said, "What in the world are you doing sitting in here doing nothing when everybody around here is breaking their necks to get finished here? I've had enough of you. Let me go sign your card so you can get the hell out of here. Don't even look back here for a job." I was stunned. I didn't expect it. I didn't argue. I don't know if I deserved it or not. I probably did. It's possible that I became oriented toward getting whatever I was doing done in a hurry, so that I could sit, smoke, and do nothing. He didn't give me much warning that I was getting on his nerves. Maybe he had just had to take a pile of crap from someone else, like his boss, and I was the guy waiting for him to unleash on. Anyway, I felt pretty odd, or maybe depressed. After I got paid from Manpower, I got a new sleeping bag and travel bag at an army surplus store.

That night started the next part of my stay in Phoenix. After Van Buren crossed over the dry riverbed as it came into Tempe, the name of the street changed, I think, into Main Street. That's where a lot of the bars were and was the main hangout with the young crowd. I couldn't go into the bars because I was eighteen, and you had to be nineteen to purchase alcohol in Arizona at that time. I imagine the minimum age now is twenty-one now, like everyplace else is. I was down on Main Street in Tempe that night after I got fired and was a bit depressed. Getting fired always did that to me. I was getting a ride back to the park when I asked the guy who had picked me up if he knew anyplace that I could crash. He went around the block, pulled up to a bar, and told me to tell a guy named Ron that he said it was okay for me to stay at the house.

There were four guys and two girls staying in a small two-bedroom house. My arrival made it five guys. All the guys, except me, were from New Jersey. There was brown-haired Paul who'd picked me up and was a good guy and intelligent. I can see Paul being a success now, because he had a confidence about him. There was blond-haired Paul, who was sort of the guru of the bunch. One of the girls was sleeping with him. We would sit around the table after dinner, smoking some opium, and he would talk about all the concerts he'd gone to and his opinion of some of them. A lot of my present tastes in music came from him and the music he listened to. The other two guys were Lenny and Ronnie.

Ronnie looked like a bodybuilder. I never saw him lifting weights or working out, so he either did it before or he just naturally looked cut. I never did really connect with Ronnie. We had conversations, and I didn't have any complaints with him; it's just that we didn't connect. I don't know if you understand what I'm talking about or not, but I think some of you know. I had a pocketknife at that time that I was using to do some carving. You remember my mention of the thumbs? Ronnie had a huge knife that was at least eight inches long. He also had a sharpening stone that I could use. I tried using it, but I couldn't seem to get the hang of getting it sharp. It's a problem I still have today. Come to think of it, I believe he got irritated with me for not wiping the oil off the stone before I put it up.

Lenny was a nice enough guy, but in a room full of people, most people wouldn't notice Lenny. He had moderately long, light-brown hair on a head that didn't stand out much. He wasn't an ass, and he didn't stick out as being real smart or real stupid. He was personable, but his personality wasn't a winning one. He wasn't a liar, a funny guy, or a good storyteller. I'm not saying any of this in a negative way; I'm just trying to describe the man. The funny thing is that Lenny is the one that I connected with the most. I liked him the best.

The two girls were Janet and Debbie, who were both from my home state. It turned out that they knew someone that I had met between my junior and senior year. They said he had turned into a total narc. It's funny because he and I had gone to a two-week course on drugs at the big state university as part of a state program on drug abuse. That was the first time that I had actually considered doing drugs, and he'd decided that he needed to become a narcotics agent. The same information was processed in two completely different ways. Janet went back home after about a week.

After I had been at the house for about a week, I was in Phoenix and decided that my old, black Converse shoes were getting a little ragged after having worn them for four months straight. So I went into a Sears, went over to the shoe section, and put on a pair of real comfortable boots. I walked around the store awhile for two reasons. One, I figured I wouldn't be as obvious if I just walked around a bit. The second reason was that I didn't have the courage to walk out. Nobody stopped me, so I finally got enough courage to walk out the door. As soon as I stepped out the door, a guy grabbed me by the elbows from behind and put me down on the ground. I was later told my mistake was that I did not get out of there fast enough. They then called the police and took me down to lockup. It turns out that they couldn't make an arrest until I walked out the door.

They held me overnight in a holding cell before they took me to the judge the next morning. The judge didn't like it that I didn't have an address, so he sentenced me to five days in the "compound." It seemed that there were two kinds of jails in Phoenix. One was called the compound, where they kept the winos, the DWIs, and petty thieves. The harder-core criminals were kept elsewhere, which I was glad about. I would imagine that Bubba was disappointed that I was at the compound, though. I think that your first time in jail should be something special. We should celebrate the anniversary of our first time every year so that we can be thankful for that educational experience.

Since the place had so many winos, one of the things they frisked you for was sugar. The story I heard was that it was the missing sugar from the wine in their diet that caused them to get the DTs. Every morning, we had oatmeal, and I didn't have any sugar. I like oatmeal, but ever since I was a kid, I would pile on the sugar. No, I don't think you understand! Piling on sugar took on new meaning with me. When I say I finally started drinking coffee with cream and sugar, I would put five or six spoonfuls in a cup of coffee. Now I had none. I know some people might argue with me on this, but I'm going to come straight out and say it: oatmeal is pretty dull without sugar. One of the guys I met in there was just in the institution at night. He was serving out his sentence for a DWI. He said they didn't frisk him, so he would get me some sugar. When he showed up with the sugar the next night, I was happy again. I put most of the sugar in my jacket pocket. When we came back from our work detail, they frisked me and found most of my sugar. I was down in the dumps again. I had to face the facts. I was "jonesing" for sugar (this is a freak term for "really craving." Heroin was also known as Jones.) It was, after all, my drug of choice. Everybody has something they can't control.

My time in the compound passed uneventfully. They let me out of jail, and I went back to the house in Tempe. They had been wondering what had happened to me. I had left my stuff, went out one morning, and didn't come back for five days. I don't think that they were exactly glad to see me, but they did welcome me back. We smoked some opium and some pot and just talked. This was the first time I had ever had opium. I didn't make me real high, but it did make me feel real mellow. Remember how often we used that term back in the seventies? Music was mellow, or the atmosphere was mellow, or a guy's personality was mellow. Quite often, *mellow* was the only word you could use to describe some things. To me, it always had a positive connotation.

Now I'm afraid to tell some of you naturalists out there what we did with the old car on the riverbed. Ronnie and brown-haired Paul had gotten hold of an old, green '53 Mercury. It had no doors or backseat. Ronnie, Paul, Lenny, and I rode it down to the riverbed between Tempe and Phoenix and used it like a dune-buggy for about an hour. Then we tried to light it on fire. It didn't burn well. Ronnie stuck a rag in the feed to the gas tank and lit it. Nothing happened. It's probably a good thing it didn't. One of us probably would have taken a piece of shrapnel in the jugular, and then we would have been in the deep poo-poo. Sorry about slipping into teacher talk. Anyway, after not really doing anything to destroy the car, we abandoned it. Now I'm going to go punk here and say it wasn't me that had an active part in this travesty to nature. I was an accessory to the fact.

There was another house that we associated with. I think there were six people living in a house that was about the same size and only about six blocks away. One night, we were heading over there for supper. I guess we were going to supply the vittles, so we went to a grocery store to pick up a few items, like everything. The only problem was that we had no money, or at least not very much. I was going to get some garlic bread, which luckily for me was close to the front door. Everybody else had a specific item to get. Blond Paul told me that I didn't have to go in and get anything, knowing that I was going to be pretty nervous after going to jail for shoplifting not too long before. I didn't feel I could not be willing to do my share, and besides, they had given me some good advice on how to not get caught. One was to get it and go. Don't walk around casually for awhile. Second, do anything you have to not to get caught. Run, fight, do whatever it takes, but don't get caught.

Anyway, it turned out blond Paul ended up getting caught trying to steal a fifth of whiskey. I guess he got cocky. I never would have had the balls to try jacking a fifth. As they were hauling him off, he said not to try and come up with bail; he was going to ride it out. The next day, he found out it was either $150 or thirty days in jail. It was in Tempe, not Phoenix, so they came up with the money. I don't really know where they got the money, but it wasn't from me.

About a week after that, someone came up with a bunch of mushrooms. I've done mushrooms about four or five times in my life, and I believe the last time was about thirty years ago, but I've always thought that mushrooms were the best hallucinogenic. They don't make you think you can fly. They are the mellowest high. Probably the best thing about them is that when you are coming down, you get the giggles. You laugh long and hard at anything. This was the first time that I ate any mushrooms.

After we ate the mushrooms, we went for a ride into the desert. There were about seven of us, and we pretty well packed a car. On the way out there, one of the girls started freaking out a little bit, and they were trying to calm her down. I didn't know her. She was the sister to somebody in the other house. So anyway, I started mocking her freaking out. I was told in definite terms to shut up. If I am remembering this correctly, I believe I deserved it. To my credit, I did shut up. I don't know where we went to be "out in the desert," but we had a fire and of course sat around for at least a couple of hours staring at each other and the fire while our minds raced out of control. The first couple of hours of a trip are usually the wildest. If you take some good shit, you will at times think that you are going to lose it. You are going to go crazy. After an hour or so, you start coming down in barely detectable ways. That's when you start thinking that you won't go over the edge. You then spend the next four or five hours coming down, bit by bit. I believe faces are the strangest things to watch. They are constantly changing, and you don't know how much of it is the acid and how much of it is the person actually changing his expression.

On the way back to the car, I was walking with the girl who was freaking out earlier. She was looking a lot better since she had come down a bit. She asked me with a nice, pretty smile on her face if I was one of the ones that was being nice to her earlier. I said no. I was thinking at that time that I might have gotten some pussy if I had been nice to her earlier. Actually, I'm thinking that I didn't really have a chance. It's no wonder I was still a virgin.

One day, I went down to the employment office to see if they had any small, temporary jobs. They had one job that was washing the outside of windows for a couple of old ladies. I said sure and went over there and did the job in a few hours and made maybe ten dollars. When I got back to the house, the guys said they were going over to some arena where Loggins and Messina were playing. They were at their peak about that time because "Your Momma Don't Dance" was at the top of the charts and getting a lot of radio time. Some of you might remember those days of AM radio when the same songs were played over and over, because it wasn't called Top 40 for nothing.

Anyway, when we got to the place, we were looking for a way to get in. Some guy said he would sell me a ticket for three dollars. Since I had few dollars that day, I could get myself and one other person in, but when I asked how the other two were going to get in, they said they would find a way. Somehow, I believed them, and I was right, because they found a way. They started up high and then worked their way up front till someone ran them out. It was a good show, and we had a good time.

As November turned into December, the residents of our house were trying to figure out how they were going to get the cash for rent. I had been contemplating heading east toward Florida. I told them that, and they didn't seem pleased. I stuck around a little while longer. I worked a couple of days doing odd jobs so that we could have a little cash around, but about the middle of December, I grabbed my stuff and started hitchhiking toward Florida. I saw Lenny at Mardi Gras a couple of months later, and he acted very indifferent toward me, like the group talked bad about me after I left. I can understand how they felt that way, because I stayed there two or three weeks and contributed nothing. He did say that the two houses had converged and survived.

C H A P T E R   7

Going to Key West

I got a ride in Tucson that got me all the way to Dallas. I was planning on taking I-10 to Florida, but the two guys driving the red van with carpet on the walls in the back were going through Dallas on I-20, and since that got me through west Texas, I went along. It was a comfortable ride, and the company was good, so why not? Since I was going to take I-10, I had to spend about a day getting from Dallas to Houston. By the time I got to Louisiana, I-10 was not completed all the way, so a good portion of driving through western Louisiana was spent on US-90.

Let me tell you a few things about the people of south Louisiana. Some of the people are not real smart. They went generations doing the same thing, which was shrimping and crabbing. Many parents didn't think it was necessary to learn how to read and write. I had never met anybody who couldn't read or write until I got to Louisiana. I know that may be derogatory to the people I love, but the people who can't read or write aren't going to be reading this, so it doesn't matter. On the other side, these people have good hearts and live good, honest lives. These people live for that old saying, live and let live." They don't try to make others live by their standards.

I was picked up somewhere near Lafayette by Fred, an oil field worker heading home to Arkansas after being offshore for three weeks.

76

It was raining pretty heavily, and it was around noon. He was driving a mid-sixties model Chevrolet. It didn't take long to see he was taking shots of whiskey straight out of the bottle. He offered me a shot almost as soon as I got into the car, and I took them because I was wet. I don't really like the taste of alcohol. I am normally a big pussy when it comes to taking direct shots of anything straight out of the bottle. I make the strangest look when I do it, and it's not the same look the cowboy makes in the movies when he comes straight off of the desert and the first thing he drinks is whiskey; however, this day, I did. I wonder from time to time if that guy ever made it home that day.

I only rode with that guy for about fifteen or twenty miles. In the interest of making conversation, as he was describing being offshore for three weeks, I asked him if he had to be a bit of an isolationist. I know now that that was a lame question to ask some redneck coming out of the oil patch, but what can I say, we can't always say something clever or be a good conversationalist. Even though I doubt many would find it funny, I was amused by his answer. He said, "No, I'm a machinist."

When the machinist dropped me off, I went into a restaurant and got something to eat. After I ate, I sat out front with a sign that said "east or Florida" and read a book. After about an hour, a woman in her mid-forties with blonde hair cut somewhat short and wearing a crocheted hat asked me where in Florida I wanted to go. I told her it didn't matter, so she asked me if I wanted a ride. The rain was letting off, and my buzz from the whiskey was shrinking. Most of the time, women did not pick up hitchhikers. I don't blame them. It was extremely rare for a woman over forty to pick someone up. Actually, that was the only time I remember that happening.

My conversation with Mary started off light and guarded. As we neared New Orleans, she said she wanted to stop off for a little while in New Orleans. We went down to what I now know as the French Quarter, or if you prefer, the Vieux Carre, and parked on Bourbon Street. It was either because it was a long time ago, or maybe it was because it was like December 21 and close to Christmas, but you don't park on Bourbon anymore. Anyway, it was about then that she pulled out her weed and said she needed a little attitude adjustment for this. She rolled a real skinny joint. It looked like it was mostly paper. However, it was good pot, and I got a nice buzz.

The atmosphere of the French Quarter is something I've never been able to get over. I still like to go down there from time to time just because there is always something to see. This was my first time, and I was in awe. Maybe that's overstating it, but I did love it. We went into a little establishment, and I ordered a beer. Mary got to talking to a wild-looking girl, saying things like, "With my brains and your motor, we could go a long way." I'm not sure I totally understand that comment, but I understood enough. I was just beginning to realize that Mary was pretty wild herself.

I started to watch the dance floor. I noticed one slightly effeminate guy that was dancing with a lot of different girls. I swear it was five minutes before I finally noticed two guys dancing together. I credit the fact that it took me so long to notice that all the couples dancing were either two guys or two girls to: 1) I was from a small town in the Midwest and had not fully become aware that gay people were out there; and 2) I was stoned. After that, I was decidedly uncomfortable thinking all these guys would be hitting on me, and I wouldn't know how to say no. That's what's called "early onset homophobia." Don't laugh. It happens to be a real disease.

Since that was the only place I knew in New Orleans, when I later planned to meet some friends from high school at Mardi Gras, Pete's on the corner of Bourbon and St. Peter was where I told them to meet me. A few years later, my older brother came to see me for Mardi Gras. On Mardi Gras day, I took him down to that corner also known as "the gay corner," mainly because there were two gay bars on that corner. It freaked him out right proper, if you ask me. To tell you the truth, I was a little surprised to see one guy sucking off (also known as "blowing") another guy on the balcony. You have to love the French Quarter, because it's not like anyplace else in the world.

Anyway, that was the only place that we went, and then Mary and I got back on the road. When we got on the interstate, we headed west. I was driving, and I was still missing my glasses. After going twenty miles in the wrong direction, we finally got headed toward Florida. Mary said she didn't really want to get a hotel room because she would feel awkward, and I felt the same way. We went by way of the old US-90 through Mississippi and Alabama. I wasn't sleepy, so I drove through the night. It was slightly raining, and there was nobody on the highway in the wee hours of the morning. We talked some of the way, but she slept most of the night. Early in the morning, she took over and drove the rest of the way.

She was going to her parents' house somewhere in the north central part of the state. How much of what she told me is true, I don't know. The life she said she led was rough. She was a practicing junkie for quite a while. She thought Sammy Davis Jr. was singing about heroin when he was singing about the "Candy Man." Maybe he was. I know she was forty-five years old and had a whole lot more experience than I did. I was really into discovery at that time. I wanted to try new things; but I knew then, and I definitely know now, that that is one life I don't want to experience. Time has a way of changing you. I still want to experience a lot of things, but I'm much more selective about what that is. Old age gets to us all.

We made it to her parents' house that evening. I don't think she was totally comfortable with this visit with her parents. Her parents were your average grandma and grandpa type of old people that had your nice, average slab house in Florida. I'm sure they didn't know everything that happened to their daughter, and I don't think she wanted them to know. I'm sure she did some stuff that they would not approve of. She may or may not have been ashamed of her life, or parts of it, but it was something they wouldn't really understand. Sometimes it's just easier if some people don't know everything about you.

I spent the night at their house and took a shower. The next day, I headed for the east coast of Florida. I took the highway south once I hit the coast. As Christmas Eve came, I started hoping a great experience would come my way. My daydreams took over. I pictured a beautiful girl picking me up, and, well, you can fill in the blanks. I sometimes wonder if other people have daydreams like mine or whether my daydreams are overly crazy. I was going to say *creative*, but I think *crazy* is a better. I sometimes feel my imagination hurts me when the reality doesn't match my dreams. You will notice that I haven't fully described my dreams. That's because when I am sitting for hours waiting for a ride or driving along, the dream changes. It gets more complicated as time goes on. I'm sorry to say that often, my dreams are about how I have impressed somebody with my adventures. Hey, I can honestly and proudly say that no daydream of mine has ever come true.

On Christmas Eve, I called my parents and talked to my family. My sister and two brothers were there, and I talked to all of them. It felt odd talking to my family on Christmas Eve but not being there. I wanted to feel left out, but I knew I couldn't. I was gone because I chose to be gone, so I couldn't exactly complain about it. It was nice, though, and I'm sure I was homesick some. Anyway, my mom told me to call a number on Christmas night because some friends from high school were going to be there and they wanted to talk to me.

When there weren't any cars on the road anymore that night, I ended up sleeping in some bushes Christmas Eve night. Some days, the adventure wasn't anything special.

On Christmas Day, I woke up, crawled out of the bushes, and headed on down the road. Once I got to Miami, I found a mission that was giving out a Christmas meal. After I had eaten a well-prepared meal, I did something I am not proud of. I started debating with one of the Jesus freaks, arguing that God didn't exist. I now consider that rude. The guy didn't take it bad, and, in fact, I think he liked the opportunity to present his opinions in a logical manner. Later on in my youth, when I took Jehovah's Witnesses into my house and tried to convert them into atheists, I figured they should be able to handle it and, in fact, deserved it, but these people in Miami went to all the trouble of getting food and preparing it for homeless people, and I think it was disrespectful of me to show off like that.

I did call my friends that night. It was great talking to them, and they were surprised to find out I was in Florida. One of my standard jokes now is when someone talks about a friend, I say that I wish I had friends. At that time, they were my friends, and I suppose I can say that they are still my friends when I see them at reunions, but I now know that when I took off and walked away from the everyday aspects of their life that I was distancing myself from them, especially since I don't keep in touch. Anyway, that night, I felt much better than I did the night before.

A couple of days after Christmas, I heard about a big concert they were having at the Hollywood Speedway. I made it there before noon and hung around. I didn't have any money, so I was just looking for a chance to get in. Finally, someone found a hole in one of the side fences and took off through it. As soon as more people saw it, about fifteen or twenty of us rushed the hole, and they couldn't shut it fast enough to keep at least a dozen of us from getting in for nothing.

There is a big advantage to getting into a concert for free. I have always had to feel like I was getting my money's worth on anything I spend money on. I suppose most of us do, yet, many of us don't have the same standards when it comes to entertainment. I have known people that will go six blocks out of the way and cross over six lanes of traffic to save themselves seventy-five cents in gas. These same people will spend an extra forty-five minutes at the grocery store to check all the prices so that they can save a couple of dollars; yet, they will spent fifty dollars at a restaurant without even blinking and spend twenty dollars tooling around in their boat because that's something they want to do. Anyway, I feel that I want to get my money's worth when it comes to having a good time. I've always thought that weed was one of the best bargains out there, because I can get many hours of enjoyment for forty or fifty dollars.

A few years back, I went to a Santana concert with my daughters, and we paid a little over fifty dollars each for the tickets. I accepted that I had to do my share to get my fifty dollars' worth, and I set to the task by talking to all my neighbors, dancing, and generally trying to have a good time. After a while, I just wasn't sure I had got my fifty dollars worth of fun yet, so I got to dancing harder and having a better time. You know, it wasn't until I was naked and dancing on the stage that I felt that I had got my money's worth. Of course, this is a joke. A couple of years ago, I was looking up prices for a Rolling Stones concert in Atlanta. The cheap seats were $150, and the good seats were fifteen hundred dollars. Can you imagine what would I have to do to get fifteen hundred dollars worth of fun? Actually, I would have to shoot for two thousand dollars worth of fun, because surely it would have to include some jail time. I can't imagine having two thousand dollars worth of fun in one night.

As I was saying earlier, there is a big advantage to getting into a concert for free, because there are no expectations and no minimum requirements that are placed on your mind because of shelling out money. It's actually easier to have fun, because you don't have the stress of *having* to have fun. If you get into a concert for free, then you would have to get the shit kicked out of you not to get your money's worth. I got my money's worth that day. In fact, I had a pretty good time.

It was a sunny day. There were stadiums on either side of the speedway, which was for dragsters. The stands were full, and the infield was also full. When one of the lesser bands was playing—I think it was some group call Roxie—there was a guy standing in the middle of the infield naked. He looked pretty fucked up. I think it took the authority figures awhile to make their way out to get the guy out of there.

I saw John McLaughlin and his Mahavishnu Orchestra, Edgar and Johnny Winter, and the Allman Brothers. It was supposed to be like ten hours of music, but it went quite late. The Allman Brothers were without Duane at that time, but they still felt a need to play for three hours. I haven't been to that many rock concerts, but this one had to be up there at the top on my list. After the concert, I just snuck off and found a place to stretch out my sleeping bag.

A couple of days before New Year's, I was dropped off in Coconut Grove in Miami at some restaurant. Out of the restaurant walked Dan from Phoenix. It had been about a month and twenty-five hundred miles since I'd seen him. I did then and do now think that was strange. Anyway, we started hanging out with each other again. He showed me his routine in Coconut Grove, but we didn't stay too long because I told him I wanted to go to Key West, and he said okay.

We got to Key West just in time for a New Year's Eve party. There was an open area on the south side of the Island, and a bunch of people were parked there having their New Year's party. That was the start of 1973. I didn't last too long that night. I laid out my sleeping bag and nodded off right after midnight with the sounds of "Jesus Is Just Alright" by the Doobie Brothers banging around in my head.

Dan and I didn't stay together very long this time. I don't really remember him deciding to leave, but I know he was gone by the fifth. When Dan and I first met, we were both inexperienced on the road. I had been on my own a little over two months, and Dan had been away from home about a month. We were innocents when we first met, and we learned the ways of the road together.

Within the three months that Dan had been on his own, he had definitely become harder and more callused. One of the ways it showed up was with panhandling. When we first got together, we used to panhandle to get cash for food. I didn't like doing it. I didn't like begging. When I did it, it was because I needed to eat. I didn't do it just so I could have some money in my pocket or because I wanted a drink. Sometimes I liked to panhandle other panhandlers. There was a guy in Key West that was always trying to get high. He was always asking people for change so that he could get a shot, or a bottle, or a hit of something. He was one of those that could not stand not to be high. Anyway, every time I saw him, I would ask him if he had any spare change. It used to piss him off.

Now, getting back to Dan, he started panhandling practically anytime he saw someone on the street. The other thing that he did was something that I didn't feel I could do. Every hitchhiker from time to time would get picked up by some guy who wanted sex from you. Dan said he didn't have a problem with letting someone suck on his dick for a few dollars. Call me old-fashioned, or call me a homophobe, but I just didn't want to do that. When you're a bum on the road, you have to believe in "live and let live." You don't really have the right to look down your nose at someone else's method of surviving. Anyway, Dan moved on after we spent a few days together, and I never saw him again.

I loved Key West. There were a lot of freaks in Key West. Most of the locals didn't appreciate us. I can't really blame them. We produced nothing, yet we didn't have any problem asking someone for a handout, or if that didn't work, there we were, stealing something from a store. For most of my stay in Key West, I didn't eat much. There was just too much competition for just a few dollars. Some times I would scrounge together a few dollars here or there, and sometimes I did a little panhandling, but quite often I did without.

Most of my meals were peanut butter and jelly sandwiches that were supplied in an old store on the main street in town by an old Christian who was trying to help and maybe convert us. I also ate a lot of coconuts. You had to be careful with coconuts, though, because eating too many of them gave you diarrhea.

At first, I spent the nights in that open area on the south side of the island. I remember waking up one morning with two other guys camping in the area. One guy had just come down from New Jersey, and the other guy was just an old bum like me. The new guy was saying that we needed to get jobs and do this right. In fact, he said that we *had* to get jobs and was very hard lined on this. I remember telling him that you don't have to get jobs to survive, and the other guy agreed with me. Well, that sure did upset New Jersey. He stormed off, and we never saw him again.

Every day ended at Sunset Pier on the west side of the island. Most of the tourist stuff was on the west side. Hemingway's home was over there, and so were all the bars and the nightlife, as was the navy base.

Whatever you did during the day, everybody would end up on the pier that faced the sunset.

After a few days, I started keeping my stuff on top of a roof that you could get to through this small park that was on Duval Street. I think the park was where a store used to be but was torn down for some reason. The rooftop sleeping place was all right until it rained for a few days, and then it wasn't so cool.

The day before my birthday, I decided to earn a little money. I went to a seafood packing plant and deheaded shrimp. It has been documented, but has not been proven categorically, that my hands are the slowest hands in the world, but, of course, I am talking about hands that don't have a mutation or have been injured in an accident. The old Cubans that were working there were popping those heads off of the shrimp at a rate of three or four baskets to my one. Oh, and the heads make your hands itch. At the end of seven hours, I made about seven dollars. That was the hardest seven dollars I ever earned.

So, the first thing I did with my hard-earned seven bucks was get something to eat. It was birthday eve, I had eaten, and I had five big, bad dollars in my pocket. The next thing that came along was that someone offered me three hits of acid for five dollars. I didn't like the fact that I was spending all my money for LSD, but I figured I could sell one of those hits for two dollars, and then I would have two hits for three dollars, or I could sell two for four dollars and have one for one dollar. It was a good plan, except for the small, inconvenient fact that I couldn't sell any. Nobody seemed willing to buy.

I woke up in the morning from my nest on the roof and walked over to the beach on the south side. I took two hits of acid and took everything off except my shorts and a hat that was open on the top and a bill out in front. I guess you could call it a visor. I sat around on the beach for a little while, but there was no one else around, and the acid had a lot of speed in it, so I started walking counterclockwise around the island. My feet are normally quite sensitive, but because of the acid,

I wasn't feeling a thing. I walked about three quarters of the way around the island and back with no shirt or shoes.

About noon or one o'clock on the east side of the island, as I was staring off into the aquamarine, crystal-clear water, I had an epiphany. It suddenly struck me with its pure simplicity. *There is no such thing as complete contentment.* That was it. That explained so much. Some people believe that if they try hard enough, they will find complete contentment. And when they don't find it, they feel cheated. Just about everybody that has taken any drugs has an idea while stoned that is phenomenal in its truth but doesn't really pan out when looked at in the cold, harsh light of sobriety, assuming that they even remember it. Now, I don't believe this one is actually that stupid when you look at it later. This idea is more of a *duh*. You know, one of those ideas that seem so true at the time, but later, when you think about it, it is so basic that it must just be one of those things everyone figures out at one point in their lives.

When I got back from my walking journey, I put a shirt on and realized that I had a sunburn on my back in the middle of January. When I got over to the other side of the island near Sunset Pier, I got to talking to some guys and traded my last hit of acid for some THC. Back in them days, everyone sold PCP as THC, which is the chemical in marijuana that gives you your buzz. Now, everyone knew it was PCP, which is horse tranquilizer, but it still was sold as something else. Anyway, the PCP which is also known as Angel Dust now days, combined with the speed in the acid to make me feel pretty good, so I was just right for a nice sunset.

Over at the pier, there were a couple of guys that were playing guitars when somebody hooked them up to electricity, and they got out their amplifiers and commenced to jammin'. It was one of the best impromptu parties I've ever seen. Amazingly enough, I don't even think they knew it was my birthday. As the sun went down into the sea and left an ever-shrinking band of gold, orange, and red followed by the deepest blue sky, we got crazy. After the guys decided to pick up their equipment and the crowd dispersed into the tropical night, I decided to go to the Christian store and get a peanut butter and jelly sandwich.

As I was strolling down Duval toward the peanut butter and jelly shop, two guys with backpacks who looked like they had just gotten there asked me what was going on. I told them about the electric guitars on the pier as the sun set. One guy asked me if things were like that all of the time there. I said that it wasn't like that all the time, but it was like that tonight. I strolled on down to the PB&J shop. After dining on Jiff and grape jelly on white, of course, I spent about an hour in the park before turning in to my sleeping bag on the roof. It was the most memorable birthday of my life.

During the next week, I called my mom and talked for a while. She offered to send some money, and since it was like a birthday, I accepted. If you've ever had somebody send you money, it's murder waiting on it. On the morning that the money was supposed to get there, I hadn't eaten in about a day and a half. I was walking around Duval Street waiting for Western Union to open up when a guy asked me if I wanted to earn a couple of bucks mopping his establishment before it opened up. Being as I was hungry, I said yes. After I earned my two dollars, I went to get something to eat. I felt like experimenting, so I ordered a squid stew. You don't know how big of a deal it is for Midwesterners to experiment with food. We like our meat and potatoes. It may have been because I was hungry and that I would have thought it was great even if it was crap, but I thought it was good.

When I got my money, I went out and made the best investment I could with the money and got some Jamaican. As I had said earlier, just because somebody says it's Columbian or Jamaican doesn't mean that it's not Homegrown in disguise; however, considering the geographical region we were in and the potency of the herb, this stuff was probably Jamaican. It was good pot. In the society that existed with the people I was hanging out with, having some pot made you popular. Pot also has great trading value. Food comes easier when you have good pot. For the next couple of weeks, the living was easy.

We had a cold spell the next week. It got all the way into the sixties, and we were miserable. One guy said his fishnet stockings that he used diving helped a lot with keeping comfortable when he wore them under his pants. On one cold and rainy day, I wanted to get indoors for a while, so I went to the library. I spent all day reading *1984*. When I got to the last fifty pages, I went outside and smoked a joint and then went back in and finished the book. I normally don't like to read while I'm stoned because it takes me so long to read anything. I have to think about everything too much. Those last fifty pages were mind-warping while stoned.

I met a guy, Roger, that was camping out with some others on the south side of the island, and I said that I would go hang out with them. I, of course, brought my pot, which, as I said earlier, makes you popular. I was sitting around the campfire rolling a joint, and one of the guys remarked that you could tell I was a guy who took pride in my work. I was busy rolling the perfect joint with my Jamaican pot with my fifty-dollar bill-rolling papers. I had gotten pretty good at rolling cigarettes, since I usually had to roll Bull Durhams or Tops. Bull Durhams came in a little bag, and the papers were small and didn't have any adhesive. They were the cheapest cigarettes that you could buy, at the hefty price of ten cents. Once you got where you could roll a smokable cigarette, you could roll anything. Anyway, the guy was right; I was taking pride in my ability to roll my joints.

I found out that several junked cars were behind a bar on Duval, and nobody minded if people camped out in them. Later on, that changed, to my detriment. At first, it was nice. The cars were late-fifties, early-sixties sedans with bench seats. Two guys could sleep comfortably and have someone to talk to until they fell asleep. I usually spent the night in a two door '61 or '62 Chevy in the back with Nick in the front. One morning, we woke up and of course started it off with a joint. I was about out by then. There went my popularity. Nick had some PCP (or was it THC?), and we took some of it.

Later, I was walking down the street in some back neighborhood I was not usually in, going toward the south shore, when I ran into Roger. I was definitely fucked up at that point. He looked pretty bad and asked me if I had any money or if I knew where he could get something to eat, because he hadn't eaten for two days. I didn't have any money, and it was way too early for the PB&J store. I then thought of that thing that Hoagy used to do. I told Roger that I didn't know if it would work, but I had an idea. We went a couple of blocks to a restaurant. I asked the waitress if the manager was around. She went into the kitchen, came back, and said he was busy but wanted to know what we wanted. I went into my spiel about how we were willing to do some work for some food. She went back into the kitchen, came back, and told us to have a seat at a table. Then she started waiting on us and asking us what we wanted to drink.

When she asked me what I wanted to eat, I asked which was cheaper, soup or chili. I was just trying to get something to eat, not take advantage of their hospitality. She told us we were not getting chili or soup but that we were getting a meal complete with salad, meat, bread, and vegetables. Afterward, we had dessert too. I was delicious. After the meal, I asked her what we could do to earn our meal, and she said there was nothing to do. I thanked her, and we left. The whole gesture was unexpected. I always wondered if there was a manager in the back at all. I sometimes wonder if she wasn't the owner of the place. It was extremely nice of her. She treated us as if we were as good as anybody else. I never tried that routine again. Maybe I didn't think of it again, or maybe I was afraid it would mess up a good memory. I also never saw Roger again.

All good things must come to an end. I had finally smoked up my beautiful Jamaican pot. It was good pot—or did I say that already? One night, somebody went to all the cars and said that new people were running the bar. The new managers had called the cops, and everybody was going to be arrested for trespassing. Nick left right away, but I hesitated for a while. When I saw the flashing lights, I had just started getting my stuff together and putting on my shoes. As the police were coming in the gate, I calmly walked out the gate and across the street to a little alley between two buildings. I thought I had gotten away. I was cold, so I got out a sweatshirt when a cop walked around the corner and told me to go with him. Obviously, I should have gone about four blocks before taking the time to put on a sweatshirt, or I should have at least taken off running.

Anyway, they took me down to the police station and booked me for trespassing. The jail had one common area with a table, some benches, a shower, some toilets, and some books. Behind the common area were four cells with four bunks in each one. I spent that first night in the common area on the table. The next day in court, I was given fourteen days in jail. I don't think the authority figures in town liked having bums hanging out in their town, and we were being told to get out of town.

While I was sitting in the courtroom waiting to be sentenced, a cop was telling the judge all the things that a guy that we called Cherokee was doing when he was arrested. He was walking around like he was completely lost. He was trying to pick something off of the rear light on the cop car. A lot of the people waiting were having a hard time not laughing out loud as the story went on. Anyway, Cherokee was sentenced to fourteen days also. He had eaten a flower around there called Deadly Nightshade. I never saw the stuff, but from what was described, I think it was Jimson Weed.

The first few days weren't too bad. We spent the nights in our bunk cell. Then they woke us up and put us in the common room for breakfast. We spent all day in the common room and then back in our bunks at night. At least, it went like that for a couple of days, but then we started getting too many jailbirds for the cage. By the end of the week, there were thirty-some prisoners being put up in a jail that was made for sixteen people. The first couple of days were nice because one of my bunkmates had put some pot down his pants, so the guys that were in my bunk cell got stoned for a few days. After three days, we had to stay in the bunk cell all the time except to go to the common room and take a shower or a crap. In my cell, there was Tom (who had the pot), Cherokee, and Dean, with whom I would spend some time once we got out. Funny thing about jail is that if there's nothing to do but read crappy books, play cards, take a shower, shoot the shit, smoke cigarettes, and eat, then you get to where you count time by when the next meal is. If I would have stayed in jail long, I would have gotten fat. The food was just okay, but when you spend your time thinking about the next meal, you get hungry, and the food tastes better.

There were a couple of trustees who got to get out and run around outside the jail. We were able to have the trustees get us some tobacco at the store. Problem was that nobody had any money. We pooled our money to get a couple of boxes of Tops. When we got down real low on tobacco, we would take all the butts and roll one cigarette. It was hard to take that one, though, because it was sort of nasty smoking a cigarette made from the butts of others. You've got to be desperate for a cigarette to smoke one of those. I guess sometimes it's just hard to suck on a nasty butt.

After about three days of being cramped up in a cell with too many people, someone found out that one of the prisoners had hepatitis, so everybody started getting real rowdy. We started yelling a bunch of crap, and a couple of guys even lit some books in the common room and a mattress on fire. I don't think anyone was really concerned with the hepatitis except for the guys in his cage with him; we just wanted to get rowdy because we were bored and there wasn't much danger. I think it stirred up the jailers, though. The next day, we got shots for hepatitis, and they started letting some prisoners out early. That is how I did my fourteen days in only seven. It was an interesting study in human nature, but I was ready to get out. When they gave me back my possessions to let me out, they saw the papers I had leftover from rolling my pot. The papers were the kind that looked like money that you get in a head shop. They knew what they were for. They told me I had better watch myself with those or I was going to find myself back in jail again, and the next time, I wasn't going to be let out early. I said okay.

After I got out, I called my mom, because I had been over that week that I was supposed to call in. I don't remember whether I told my parents about that little spell in jail or not. I might have told them about this time, but I know I didn't tell them about Phoenix.

I ran into Dean when we got out. We went to get something to eat, and then we scored some pretty good acid. We went down to Sunset Pier and let the stuff kick in. After the sunset, we started walking down to the action on Duval Street. Just as I was approaching Duval, I noticed someone acting very strange, slinking around in the shadows, but I didn't think about it much. After I turned on to Duval and was about a half a block down, I heard footsteps running down the sidewalk behind me. When I turned around, the crazy guy hit me right in the mouth and started taking off my shirt. I didn't fight back. In fact, I reacted instinctively. I grabbed my shirt and took off running and didn't stop for at least a block.

The guy didn't hurt me, but I was in shock. I had not been in a fight in three years. I know it seems unlikely that I would be out on the road and be in plenty of undesirable places and never have to fight, but I've always had a charmed life. I haven't always gotten all I wanted, but I've had very little real bad luck. So anyway, between the fact that I was cooking pretty good on acid and the fact that I hadn't been in any fights, I was freaked out. I couldn't believe it, and my mental state was allowing me to think all sorts of crazy thoughts. Maybe the guy was tripping on the same acid we were.

We roamed on down Duval as the night went on. We stepped into a bar where two guys were playing and performing. It seemed amazingly quiet as they performed. The audience was sitting and listening but wasn't reacting in any way, so I started howling and whooping. It's funny, but the crowd starting reacting in the same way. For a place that was so quiet when we went in, it got rowdy in a hurry. I blame myself.

After midnight, a guy picked us up where Duval meets Truman. We didn't really want to go anywhere in particular, and I don't think the guy had anyplace that he wanted to go. We rode around with him for awhile. He was in his late twenties or early thirties and was driving a Continental. At one point, the conversation turned to what a weird night we were having and I made the comment that some guy had beat the shit out of me. All right, I overreacted a bit. The guy turned around from the front seat to look at me. He was probably thinking that I looked all right for someone that had had the shit beaten out of him.

He said that earlier, he was sitting on a bench and decided to smoke a joint. I got the impression that he didn't smoke pot unless it was a party or something. I felt like he was looking for an excuse to smoke at that time. I said, "Why not?" He turned around and said, "Exactly! Why not?" He said it like he had had an epiphany. Notice how attached I have become toward that *epiphany* word. Once I pay good money for a word, I like to use it. I had a student one time tell me that she had an epiphany. I told her that they made a cream that would clear it right up. She liked that joke. Sometimes the best epiphanies are short and to the point.

He gave off the impression that he'd been raised with money. For some reason, Dean wanted to hook up with him long term. He said he was leaving for Los Angeles the next day. Dean did a lot of talking trying to get the guy to take us with him. I wasn't sure I wanted to go so badly, but then again, it might be an adventure. In the wee hours of the morning, he dropped us off somewhere near where he picked us up earlier and said he would meet us the next day at a certain place on Duval.

We wondered down to South Beach and watched the sunrise. It was a good one. There were enough thick cumulus clouds scattered in prominent places in the sky to provide an ample medium for the sun to paint an enormous color storm. The fact that we were tripping on acid only made it more intense. Even though I have given a wonderfully creative description, the real thing was better.

Dean and I went to the place we were to meet the guy with the Continental, but he never showed. I wasn't surprised and sort of thought it would be a bad move from my perspective, because what was I going to do on a trip all the way to Los Angeles with no money? Was he going to pay for everything? I don't believe Dean had much. Dean seemed pretty disappointed. I guess he thought that this would be a good opportunity for him to get the right contacts. I didn't see it happening.

C H A P T E R 8

A Quest Accomplished

Somehow, my little stint in jail made me feel I was ready to leave Key West. I don't know what happened to Dean, but we went our separate ways. I started hitching out of the Keys, and when I got to Miami, I cut across the Everglades to the western coast of Florida. When I got to Fort Meyers Beach, I ran into Dean again. I hung around there for a couple of days. One evening, after we had had something to eat, we were walking out toward a secluded section of the dunes where we were camped. By we, I mean a guy named John, Dean, and I. John was pretty young, possibly in his early twenties. "The one thing I regret the most right now is that it took me so long to get my first piece of ass," said John. "I was a virgin until I was eighteen."

"I know what you mean," said Dean. "I was eighteen myself when I did it for the first time. How old were you?" he asked me. I find my reaction to that question so weird. Yes, I was ashamed of the fact that I hadn't lost it yet. So instead of being gutsy enough to admit that I hadn't ever had sex with a woman or lie and make up some age, I said nothing. They walked down the road with me and looked at me like I was going to give them an answer. I felt too awkward to say anything. I guess indirectly I did answer the question, because they didn't pressure me to answer it. I believe they knew.

When I left Fort Meyers Beach, I sort of moseyed up the coast toward Tampa. I was beginning to get tired of the road. The adventure wasn't as exciting as it used to be. I also realized that getting off the road wasn't easy. First of all, it is hard to get a job if you look like a bum. First impressions are hard to overcome if you look like hell. Second, holding down a job is hard if you have no food for two weeks until you get your first paycheck. Third, if you have no place to live, then it is hard to take showers, etcetera. Even today, when a person panhandles me, I give him some money and know that he probably couldn't hold down a job if he had one. When I hear someone tell a panhandler to "get a job," I think that shows an ignorance of that person's situation. Don't get me wrong; I know there are some people who panhandle and are bums because that's what they want to be. It may be that most bums would not hold down a job even if you set them up with an apartment and food. I do know that to tell a man to get a job when he asks for some spare change is a useless comment. You can give him some money or not, but the comment changes nothing. That guy is not going to go get a job just because you told him to.

I had taken on the habit of asking people if they knew of a place where I could crash. It's a vague term, but it is surprising how many people are willing to accommodate you for a little while. Sometimes it landed me in some peculiar circumstances. One old guy in his sixties let me stay overnight with him one night because I think he was hoping it would turn into sex, but it didn't. There were some times that I took advantage of their hospitality. One time, a guy's sister offered his apartment for me to crash in, and then the next day, I just stuck around. I made no pretense to leave, and he was too nice to tell me to get out. I laid around and read all day. I left on my own the next day.

I got a ride from a young guy named Brian and another guy in Clearwater, and, of course, I asked if they knew of anywhere I could crash. Brian said I could stay with him. He had a lot of character and personality. When they picked me up, they were just getting off work on Friday, and they stopped so that Brian could get some ouzo. I believe he is the only person I know that drank ouzo. He took me to a party that night. He told me a couple of times that I could take a shower at his house. He lived with his parents. I was going through a phase where I didn't take showers very often. Now I get to feeling very grungy after a couple of days, but at that point, I was going weeks. I know I felt awkward taking a shower at his parents' house, but that wasn't the only reason.

I hung out with him for a couple of days. He was quite generous for a guy his age who hadn't been in a similar state. On Saturday night, he had tickets to go to a Neil Young concert, and he had made arrangements for me to hang out with some of his friends. On Sunday, I called my mom for my weekly communication and found out that she had mailed a package for me to Key West general delivery, so I decided to head back to Key West. Brian dropped me off on the highway on his way to work. I liked Brian, but I don't think he was very impressed with me.

I was in good spirits when I started traveling south toward Key West, I guess because I did like my stay in Key West, and it sort of felt like going home. That feeling was enhanced by the joint that one of my rides had kindly shared with me. In fact, I caught two rides in a row where someone wanted to smoke a joint with me, and the second one had me roll one up to take with me for the road. Along about afternoon, three guys and a girl in an old, green '62 Rambler picked me up. They were just headed south with no particular place to go, and when I said I was going to Key West, they decided to check it out.

Lindy, the girl, wasn't bad-looking, but she wasn't exactly beautiful. She was about twenty-one or twenty-two and had long, dark hair and a round ass with ample tits. She was mainly from Michigan, among other places, and was attached to Ronnie, who was also from Michigan. The other two guys, Steve and Randy, were also from Michigan and flew down together to Tampa. They bought the car in Tampa and picked up Lindy and Ronnie along the way.

So there I was in a car with two pairs of Michiganians. They did not know each other until that day. I'll say this about Michiganians, they weren't all bogus. *Bogus* was a phrase that I only heard Michiganians use. That is, until I saw *Bill and Ted's Excellent Adventure.* It means "bad or wrong." For example, I could say, "The people who run the banks nowadays are bogus." Randy was learning how to play the guitar and wasn't too bad at playing some Allman Brothers. At least he had good taste in music. I got on their good side by striking up that joint that I'd been given earlier.

On the second night of our trip, we got quite a way into the Keys by evening. We decided to pull off the road and spend the night sort of camping out. The old Rambler had the front seat lay down so that the front seat to the back became one reasonably nice bed. I said I was going to sleep outside. Since it wasn't raining, I didn't see any reason why not. Boy, was I wrong. The mosquitoes were the worst I have ever seen. The people in the car had to roll up their windows, and they all voted to let me into the car. They sort of had to because of the crying I was doing. I was trying to be brave, but those little bastards were tearing me up.

The car had just enough room to lay four people side by side. A fifth person made it crowded. At first, I was down by their feet. I guess that's what I got for crying like a little girl. Five people in a car with the windows rolled up in seventy-five-degree weather for hours made it definitely stuffy. Everybody had their shirts off, including Lindy. So to make a long story short, in the course of the night, my face came up eyeball to nipple with Lindy's boob. Yeah, I know, that's not such a big deal in the grand scheme of things, but it was a big deal to me at the time. Let's just say it got me to thinking. I never did figure out why we didn't just go somewhere else to get away from the mosquitoes.

. We didn't stay long in Key West, and not too long after that, Ronnie called home and had to go back. We dropped him off at an airport in Miami, I think. That meant there was a three-way struggle between three guys and one girl. Thinking back on it, I don't believe it would have bothered Lindy to have fucked all three of us, but it didn't work out that way. Randy immediately got the inside track because he had the car and the guitar. That sounds poetic. He had the car and the guitar. He also seemed to have a source of money back home that he could tap from time to time. One night, after Randy got some money from home, we got a motel room with two beds. Steve and I were in one bed, while Randy and Lindy were in the other. There was some action going on in one bed, but it wasn't ours. It's not really easy to listen to fucking going on in the bed next to you and not be able to do anything about it.

We didn't stay in motels often. We spent several nights sleeping in the car in the lot of an all-night gas station. The guy who worked nights there didn't mind having us there. As the days went on, Lindy became bolder and bolder about letting me know it was me that she liked. One morning, we were sitting in the backseat with a blanket over us while Steve and Randy were in the front. I had my hand in her pants under the blanket, fingering her to orgasm. She said she had never had an orgasm in normal sex. She always had to get off using a finger. She liked it. Steve and Randy got out at a rest area, so Lindy took my dick out and played with it. She looked at the big veins in my dick and said that she would love to shoot some Jones right into that vein. I had never shot anything up, but from what I heard about it, I guess that would have made me an addict in a hurry.

For some reason, Randy didn't put up much of a fuss when Lindy just started to pay me more attention. One night, she gave me a blowjob in the bathroom at the gas station. The next night, we went to see *The Poseidon Adventure* at the drive-in. When we got out of there, we went back to the gas station. The attendant said that there was a travel trailer sitting for the night and that we could sleep in there. Lindy and I went in first, while Steve and Randy stayed in the car. When I finally put my dick in her for the first time, I thought I had died and gone to heaven. It was one of the few times that the experience was better than what I anticipated it to be. So often, events in your life don't live up to what you expect them to be. The concert isn't as much fun as you thought it would be, or the steak doesn't taste as good as you thought it would be. This was different. From that moment on, I believed in that old Chinese saying: "Panties may not be best thing, but they next to best thing."

Randy and Steve had gotten jobs as laborers at a big construction site. I was working through Manpower because they paid every day, so we had some cash until they got their first paychecks. I also bought a pair of shoes and a jean jacket. The shoes replaced my old, black Converse tennis shoes that I had been wearing nonstop since September when I lost my boots. I had wanted a jean jacket for a long time. I had also started taking more showers and was generally cleaner.

By the time that Steve and Randy started getting a paycheck, it was getting to be about a little over a week before I was to meet my high school friends at Mardi Gras. Lindy was saying that she wanted to get back to where her mom was living with her daughter and sister in Virginia Beach. I don't know at what point during this trip that I found out about her daughter, and I'm sure that back then, I didn't think it was that bad. But now I wonder how she could just take off for two or three weeks and leave the child with her mom. Anyway, Lindy and I decided to part ways with Randy and Steve and head up to Virginia.

I always felt that that old Rambler sure had some strange human dynamics. I wondered for a long time why they let us hang around after it became me and her. I'm not sure why they let me hang around the whole time, because I didn't bring much to the table. Sometimes I think they were too nice to tell us—or just me—to get the hell out of there, but I didn't feel like they wanted us to leave. If I talked to those two today, I'll bet they were glad I took Lindy off their hands. Maybe they wanted me around for that reason. Maybe I was too dense to get the hints, but I don't think so, because I usually understand when someone doesn't want me around.

C H A P T E R   9

My Wonderful Travels with Joe

I don't think it took us much more than a day to get up to Virginia Beach. I believe we caught a ride straight through the night through the Carolinas. Lindy's mom was probably more attractive in her day than Lindy was. By all outward appearances, they may have seemed like a normal family. There was no father figure anywhere around. The mother took care of the baby for the most part and didn't seem to care what the daughters did. She was quite liberal. I stayed with Lindy in her bed the three days I was there and she didn't have a problem with it, or at least she didn't say anything. By today's standards, that is not all that odd. In those days, that was not acceptable.

It was late February in Virginia, and the weather wasn't cold, but it was wet and dreary. I enjoyed seeing that part of the country. I had only been in Virginia one time, when I was in fifth grade. I was supposed to meet my friends in New Orleans on the Friday before Mardi Gras, which is on Tuesday. That year, Mardi Gras was in the last week in February. That meant that I would have to leave on Thursday. I knew that Lindy wanted to either go with me, or better still, she wanted me to stay. She really liked me at that time, but I wasn't ready for what she had to offer, so I left. I made it to Richmond by midday on Thursday. In Richmond, I was picked up by a green, fairly new, full-sized GM van. The driver,

Joe, had dark, curly hair and a beard. He was from New York and was half Irish, half Puerto Rican. All the way down the road, he picked up every hitchhiker he could and told them the same story. He had just been ripped off on the way down here, and if there was any way that they could chip in a few bucks for gas, it would be greatly appreciated.

By the time we got to Atlanta there was just Ken and I left in the van. Ken was about twenty-eight, had long, brown hair, and was a psychology student. We got to Atlanta late in the evening, about ten or eleven o'clock. We went down into the middle of town looking for a cool place to hang out. We had heard of some places, but I don't think we found them. At one point, we were downtown walking around when we approached a group that appeared to be some lowlifes. At that time, Ken decided that he needed to place himself between Joe and I and the group of thugs. I believe he wanted to put on a show of protecting us because he wanted us to know he knew karate. I think he wanted to establish himself as the wise guru of the group. It was an image he never fully accomplished.

Joe had the best ability to get invited to a party with complete strangers that I have ever known. At one point, we were downtown wondering if any of the lowlifes were dangerous, and a little while later, we were at someone's house having a party and taking showers. When we left the party, it was about four in the morning. We had been given instructions to get back on the interstate and were about to get on when a cop car's lights started flashing right behind us. We pulled over. Joe was driving, I was in the passenger seat, and Ken was in the back. The cop got out of his car on high alert with his gun out, yelling to get out of the car with our hands up. It was the only time I went through the complete "put your hands on the car and spread 'em" routine so often seen on TV. Even when I had been arrested and sent to jail, I didn't get the "hands on the car and spread 'em" song and dance. The cop was pretty nervous until he got us in the back of his car. Now it was our turn to be nervous.

It was while we were in the back of the police car that young Joe elected to tell us that the van had been stolen in New York. Something like that tends to make your sphincter spasm. I did not want to go to prison, and I picked up those same vibes from the others. It's one thing to go to some small local jail for a few days, but it is quite another to go to prison for car theft. I know you are just dying to find out if I did indeed go to prison and if so, how my butt cherry held out, but as it turned out, they didn't have any record of a stolen green van from New York in their system. In those days, there weren't that many computers, and they were definitely not all hooked up. They were just beginning to find out what they could do with those things. Joe says that he worked with some organization in New York that took care of consolidating the data for New York City, but they were a long way from hooking up beyond a regional grid. It turned out that there was a report of a van similar to ours that had been involved in a shooting in one of the small towns around there. That was why he was so crazy. So anyway, we were back on the road feeling light and bouncy after crapping our pants earlier. We got on the road just in time to hear Joe's and my favorite song for that trip, "Dead Skunk in the Middle of the Road." I never hear that song anymore.

We started tripping along toward New Orleans and the big Mardi Gras party. I don't think Joe was planning on going to Mardi Gras, but that's only because he wasn't planning anything. I don't know what made him just decide one day to rent a van and take off for the south, which is just the direction he steered the van. If he understood that this was burning the bridges behind him, he didn't say anything. I'm thinking now that I should have asked, but he probably wouldn't have told me the truth. With some people, you can't tell if they are lying or not, but it didn't take long to realize that most of what Joe told you was going to be altered in some degree. I don't think he cared whether you knew he was lying or not. He was blowing with the wind.

Ken, on the other hand, was supposedly heading toward his house around St. Petersburg, Florida, and was hitchhiking in the first place because he had lost his money for airfare. However, when we started toward New Orleans, he said okay. I was just beginning to see Joe's magic when it came to handling others. We stopped at a gas station in Mississippi, and he took that opportunity to con some guy out of eleven dollars under the promise he was going to send him the money if the guy would give Jim his address. It's a good thing that Jim didn't have an evil nature. He just wanted a few dollars to get to the next party.

We found our way into New Orleans about mid afternoon. If you have never been to New Orleans during Mardi Gras, you have to understand first that the people of New Orleans take great pride in their ability to throw a party. They have more experience at it than anyplace else in North America. They throw this huge party every year that draws millions of extra visitors. Besides Mardi Gras, they also host a large bowl game and are known for hosting big events, like Super Bowls. There is something for everybody, with dozens of parades where the riders on the floats throw presents to the people on the street. Now, granted, the presents are cheap plastic beads and doubloons, but you wouldn't believe how you start to get worked up at parades waiting for someone to throw you some cheap set of beads. The parades are all over town for weeks ahead of the big party on the Tuesday before Ash Wednesday.

The really heavy partying goes on in the French Quarter, and being as this was the Friday before Mardi Gras, the Quarter was packed. It had the feel of people who want to have a good time. That was the night I met Mick, William, and Lucy. We met on Decatur Street and started wondering toward Bourbon near St. Louis Cathedral. When we got to the small grocery store on Royal, Mick and William went in to get a pint of Jack Daniels. They had each had about two swallows when a cop came up and took the bottle away from them. He informed them that bottles were not allowed in the quarter and then poured it out on the ground. Mick, who was also a con man and had the capability to captivate people, but not as well as Joe, started talking to the cop like a regular guy. He said stuff like, "Oh, no. We was just having a drink, getting ready for Mardi Gras. Don't you want us to have some fun?" The cop then started acting like a regular guy and said stuff like, "I definitely want you to have some fun, but you can see what this place would be like if too many bottles turned up in these streets." It was the first time I saw how treating a cop like a person will more likely get you treated like a person.

We went on down to where I was supposed to meet my friends. Time passed, and nobody showed up. I never did see any of them that Mardi Gras. When I had figured out that I wasn't going to see any of them, we headed back to Decatur Street, where the van was. By the time we got there, I was pretty wasted. Lucy took a liking to me. For some reason, she really got off on a guy that was so drunk he was helpless. They took us back to the apartment they were living in. Once again, Joe had worked his magic. It was nice to know someone that was a con artist.

The apartment was in an old section near City Park and Bayou St. John. It is now one of the nicer parts of New Orleans. Back then, it was just a nice, quiet neighborhood. I'm guessing that the people in that neighborhood hated having us staying there. We were just a bunch of hippies. But we probably weren't the worst in their opinion, because about two blocks away was a house owned by the same Hare Krishnas that were pestering people at airports with their clothes that looked like orangeish-yellow sheets and hair that was shaved except for one spot on their heads that they let grow long. I lived in that apartment for almost six months. Most of my memories of that place are good ones.

The next day was Saturday, and we set out to start the party. We had a van, and if we picked up enough people, we were able to find some cash for gas. It got to be a standard phrase when someone got in that somebody would ask them if they had some spare cash because we got ripped off on the way down and would appreciate it. Remember, in those days, gas was about thirty cents a gallon. It didn't take much effort to keep the van rolling.

I went back to where I was supposed to meet up with my friends. Again, they didn't show up, and I was separated from Joe and the van. I got out of the van because I saw Lenny from Phoenix and I wanted to talk to him. He didn't seem too glad to see me, and I guess I know why.

I ended up on the Moon Walk at one point. The Moon Walk was on the Mississippi by Jackson Square. Everybody was going there to get stoned. There were lots of little groups of people sitting out on the rocks, smoking whatever they had. Back in the old days, there were no open areas on the river because there were warehouses all along it, but in 1962, a ship ran into a warehouse, so they tore it down. It just happened to be right alongside Jackson Square and the Café du Monde, so they left it open to the river and named it the Moon Walk after then mayor Moon Landrieu. Anyway, it was nice that it created a place where we could smoke.

At the top of the levee was a sidewalk. I was standing there when two guys with short hair came up to me and asked me if I could get them some acid. They couldn't score any because since they were in the navy and had short hair, nobody trusted them. You may be tired of the phrase, but back in them days, you had to have long hair to be a freak, and if you were in the armed forces during the time of Vietnam, you were of a different mindset. Now, this is the weird part. As I went down among the rocks and started asking if anybody had some acid to sell, one group said no, but why don't I take a hit of hash? I said great and took a toke. As I started to cough uncontrollably, I made the chunk of their hash jump out of the pipe onto the rocks. Boy, did they freak out. Boy, did I feel small. Of course, I slunk out of there right quick. I hope I said I was sorry. I probably ruined their fun for the night. All right, maybe it wasn't that weird. It turns out that I never did find any acid for the poor fellows. They weren't able to have all the fun that they had wished for.

I wondered back through the Quarter and ended up standing on the corner of Dauphine and Esplanade waiting for a bus to get me back to the apartment, and along came the old green van loaded down with people. Larry, another guy from the apartment, and I got in. We spent a couple of hours driving people around and then went back to the apartment. By that time, there must have been fifteen or twenty people crashing at the apartment.

I woke up the next morning earlier than everybody else. I was in a chair in the living room. I heard someone laughing in the dining room, even though it wasn't set up as a dining room. I mean, there wasn't a table. A girl in her teens with frizzy hair (a result of getting an Afro not long in the past) was sitting on the windowsill pouring coffee out onto the ground and laughing when it hit the ground. It turns out that she was stressed out because Mick, William, and Lucy had asked a bunch of people up to the apartment that she and Lucy had rented out. This isn't what she had envisioned for her first apartment. Right then, I should have known that she was off her rocker and left, but I didn't. Instead, I went to talk to her. After all, she was a female, and you know how we guys get when we are in the presence of females. After all, I had just lost my virginity, and I needed practice. Her name was Jonnie.

That afternoon, there was a free concert by the Allman Brothers in City Park. We got in the van and headed on over. We parked the van quite a ways from where the concert was. Somebody came along in a pickup and everybody got in except Jonnie. She wondered off into the oaks on the side of the street. I started to get in but at the last second didn't. I went over by Jonnie. As I was talking to her, I was standing in an ant pile. Jonnie told me that I was standing in an ant pile, to which I replied, "Ants don't bother me much." The ants that used to hang out in my neighborhood when I was a kid were a different kind of ant than the ants in the ant pile I was standing in. Fire ants didn't exist in my hometown. I immediately realized the flaw in my analysis of the situation. My dance of the ant had such flare and style that Jonnie immediately fell in love with me. We walked around all afternoon and never did make it to the concert.

After the concert, we all hopped into the van and spent the evening in the Quarter. Before we went to the quarter, I gave Jonnie the best kiss I had in me. She looked at me strangely, like she had never been kissed like that before, and of course, I thought it must have been good. Later, when we got back to the apartment, we were all sitting around the living room shooting the shit, which was all we could do, since there wasn't a TV. Jonnie came into the room, took my hand, and led me into her bedroom. Jonnie was one of only two people that had their own room since she and Lucy originally rented the apartment. Part of the reason she was acting so strange that morning was because she was stressed out over all the people that were staying there. Inviting all those people was not her idea. While we were in the bedroom, Nick knocked on the door. When he saw me in her bed, he got a very strange look and left. I didn't find out till later that he had been sleeping with her up till that night. He was a dick to me for a long time after that night.

Jonnie and I spent all our time together for the next few days. On Mardi Gras day, we of course went to the Quarter and walked around and looked at the freaks. Mardi Gras in the Quarter was always a freak show. There are all sorts of people dressing up in all sorts of costumes. The costumes range from very comical, like a guy walking around in a trench coat with a flexible hose and wig head at the end of the hose coming out of the bottom of his trench coat to the wildest, most intricate costumes worn by the drag queens. The Quarter means freedom for a lot of people to do anything they want to. After all, you have to be behaving pretty strangely before anyone around there was going to treat you like a weirdo. As we were walking away from Jackson Square on St. Phillip right next to St. Louis Cathedral, the cops were stuffing a naked man into one of their cars. As we walked by, everybody was harassing the cops, as if they should leave the poor naked man alone because he was just trying to have some fun. I walked by and tapped the car.

Now is a good time to explain the mentality of a policeman on Mardi Gras day in the French Quarter. By that day, they have put in all sorts of overtime and have seen just about every conceivable inappropriate act in the imagination of man. Their nerves are on a short fuse. When I tapped that car, the nearest policeman just snapped. He was heading right toward me and Jonnie, and we were backing up as fast as we could. Right when he was about to grab me, he saw Jonnie with me and grabbed the guy right next to me. We decided it was a good idea for us to get the hell out of there. It was a good time, I thought.

Ken said to me one morning that he had noticed that Jonnie and I were spending a lot of time together. I replied that we were having fun together. Jonnie was, and is, pretty smart. She's not as smart as she used to be now, because the years are kicking her butt. Today, she would be classified as gifted. She was in a program in high school where the smart kids were put into independent study and given a lot of freedom toward their own learning. It failed. Very few kids learn on their own. I suppose that if I were in school now, I would be classified as gifted, but I was not put into the smart class because I was too slow. They were just starting to put the smart kids in their own classes in those days. When I was young, most first impressions of me were not good as far as my intelligence was concerned. Most people thought I wasn't very bright. Jonnie saw through that immediately—which is a good thing, because she never had much patience for stupid people.

We stuck around another couple of days after Fat Tuesday and continued partying. The idea behind Mardi Gras is that you get wild and crazy for a while, but then Lent starts on Ash Wednesday, which starts a period before Easter in which you sacrifice something. We weren't good Catholics, and we didn't sacrifice something. We all went to the blood bank and sold our blood. I wonder how many people got stoned off of the blood given to them, because the guy who sold it right after Mardi Gras was still stoned when he sold it.

We also had an accident with the van during the celebration. Joe was driving through the narrow streets of the Quarter, and the back sliding door was open. Jim got too close to a parked car on the right side of the street and knocked the door off. They didn't stick around to find the owner of the car. I don't think it was hurt as bad as the van was. They stopped, went back, and got the door, and then we took off.

The only proper way to replace a door on a stolen van was with a stolen door. I was traveling with a pack of thieves at that point. Lanny was quite respectable in a group of thieves. They decided that they were going to go down to a used car lot on Canal at night, jump the fence, and steal a door off of another van. I didn't go with them because basically, I was a lousy thief.

On the Friday after Mardi Gras, we decided to go to Florida. After all, we had to take Ken home. I explained to Jonnie that I would be coming back. I don't know what was wrong with her, but I don't think she believed me. I suppose most girls have been told something like that in their lives that didn't come true. So anyway, Ken, Joe, Lanny, Tony, and Nancy, who was presently hooked up with Tony, and I took off for Florida, picking up all hitchhikers along the way.

Back to Florida, or More Travels with Joe

So we headed toward Florida, picking up every group of hitchhikers and, of course, giving them the spiel about needing money to get home. In Mississippi, we pulled into a rest area, put our new, stolen van door on, and dumped our old door. The only problem was that the door was white, while the van was green. We decided to spend the night on the beach at Panama City. Even though we had given our "we need gas money" routine to everyone, we were still short on cash.

We were getting by on food by making sure that all of us went into the small stores that we stopped at. That way, there were too many of us for people to keep their eyes on all of us. While we were in a store, everyone would shoplift at least something. Lanny, Tony, and Joe were the best at stealing. I wasn't good at it because I would get too worked up to do it well. To be a good thief, you have to not care about the consequences to both you and the people you are stealing from. We ate a lot of sardines in them days. Every store had sardines, and they fit into your back pocket like a wallet. I liked the ones in mustard sauce or tomato sauce best.

We used to always get a bargain at the gas pumps. In those days, about half of the stations were the kind that had an attendant come out and serve you by filling the tank and washing the windshield. The pumps had a lever on the side, and all you had to do was switch it over, and it would clear what was on the pump. Even if it was self serve, the pumps were the same. As those pumps wore out in the seventies, they were replaced with pumps that had to be cleared on a control board inside. Self serve became the norm. For us, that lever was switched over at least once before the pump cut off due to someone flipping it when nobody was watching.

When we were in Panama City, we pulled over, threw a newspaper machine in the back of the van, and took off for the beach, where we had all the time we needed to break it open and get the change out. I had seen a lot of stealing since I had been on the road, but it was usually kept in check by the fact that 1) most guys out on the road were not interested in a lot of material gains; and 2) because often, when you are by yourself, you don't feel as brave. There became a group bravado in the van. Even though most didn't know the van was stolen, the underlying mentality that emanated from Joe was that anything went, and everyone felt that they needed to do their share to keep the community, which was the people in the van, going. The more it happened, the braver everyone got.

That first night on the beach, we had a party. We had picked up two young girls that day, Charlotte and Robin. Of course, I wanted to see if I could get some more pussy since I thought I was just getting the hang of coming on to a girl. I set my sights on Robin.

She was attractive, although quite skinny. I sat next to her around the campfire. Robin seemed to like to attach herself to some guy whenever she was in a group situation, perhaps as a survival technique. There weren't many girls on the road. It had to be a rough existence for a girl. For a girl by herself, she would probably have to be fighting off some guy about 75 percent of the time. I would imagine that for most of them, the easiest way to cut down on that is to have a guy at all times. All they have to do is find the guy that doesn't turn them off and decide that they would like to fuck him. By flipping a small switch in their mind that this wasn't bad, they survived. Of course, I'm looking at this from my point of view. It's very possible that they just plain liked fucking different guys. Over the years, I have developed an opinion that girls don't really like fucking like guys do, because so few have acted like they want to fuck me. I may be right, but I'm probably underestimating their desire to fuck.

So anyway, Robin didn't seem to have a problem with me, and I seem to have the inside track. Right about then, Ken wanted to talk to me, so we went off by ourselves and talked. Ken was not too happy with the atmosphere of all the stealing that was going in the van. This adventure, I believe, had been big in his life. He had been talking for the entire week about a girl he had back home and that they had been getting real serious. Maybe this was his last chance to sow a few wild oats. Anyway, in his mind, the adventure was going sour.

Of course, I didn't have any good advice, because I was feeling the same thoughts, but it wasn't festering in me yet. I was still having a lot of fun, and I had become quite flexible mentally over the last six months. The things that would have freaked me out when I first started were just a little bit more ordinary now. Ken was showing his dissatisfaction by being irritable. We all had noticed and commented about his growing foul mood.

When we got back to the campfire, Lanny had jumped in my spot. Oh well, it was probably for the better. It turned out that Robin was only fifteen. Lanny and she were a pair for the rest of the time we were traveling together.

We dropped Ken off at his house in St. Petersburg. I think he had a lot of explaining to do to some people in his life. His last words were that he was going to write a book about his week on the road. If he wrote it, I didn't read it. That's a shame, because I always wanted to see myself as a character in a book.

We were traveling in a pack. As I said earlier, there is power in traveling in packs. For me, I liked being a part of the pack because I had traveled a long time by myself, and I was tired of it. I suppose the others felt that we could get all of what we needed—and most of what we wanted—if we worked as a group. I don't really know what the others were thinking. There's a good possibility that they had been in a similar situation themselves and were also feeling the power of the group.

We traveled on down the west coast of Florida, taking our time and seeing every beach and hangout for our kind. Like I said earlier, Joe was very good at finding a party somewhere and getting invited to it. People liked showing him a good time. Since he and I knew each other the best, I was right there when he went to partying. I guess I was having too good of a time to worry about consequences.

During most of my time on the road, I had been by myself. I thought a lot about a lot when I was by myself. Now I was part of a group in which I was readily accepted as a member. I guess that time gave me the experience to understand how cults develop. People will do anything to be part of a group, especially if they hadn't been a part of a group before. I would imagine that most cults were made up of former loners that discovered the power of the group.

One evening, we picked up a couple. The first impression the girl created was of being cheap, yet wild. It didn't take long to tell she was willing to do just about anything at just about anytime. The guy looked like a surfer bum at first, with his long, blonde hair and the way he was dressed, but he was also effeminate. So I guess we picked up a gay surfer dude and his wild-ass "fag hag." In the course of events, Joe wasn't driving, and I was all the way back by the rear door near the gay surfer dude. Since the van only had seats in the front, the rest of it was filled with sleeping bags rolled out. Everybody just either sat up or laid out.

The gay surfer dude and I were laid out parallel to the back door. Toward the front from us were Joe and the wild woman. After awhile, I noticed that she ended up on top of Joe and was fucking him. I don't believe that you could call it anything other than *fucking*. It definitely wasn't making love. She got on top of a guy she had only known for an hour or so, hiked up her dress, took his dick out of his pants, and stuck it in her. I stand corrected; she put her mouth down there first and warmed it up. So they sort of got this motion going with a slow, just passing time, type of rhythm. I felt awkward. Excuse me if I'm old-fashioned, but every time I'm laying somewhere while someone else is fucking not far off, I feel awkward. This went on for a few minutes, maybe five. I was trying to act like I didn't see anything, and nobody else was saying anything. Finally, I had to say something, so I said, "That reminds me of a washing machine."

Now, I know that wasn't the cleverest thing to say at the time; however, I wasn't the only one that felt awkward, so everybody cracked up. Things happened to Joe that never happened to me. All Joe could do was laugh and point his finger at me. About an hour later, we dropped the gay surfer dude and the wild-ass fag hag off on the highway at night, and they made their way to their destination. Immediately after dropping off the strange couple, the group in the front asked if the activities in the back had actually happened. Even though we had begun to accept anything as possible, they were still surprised at that development.

We finally made it down to Key West. I saw some people I knew, but not many. Nobody seemed really glad to see me again, because when I was staying there, I was always on my own. I remember hanging out and doing stuff with a bunch of different guys, but we didn't stay together long because I guess I was on my own adventure, and most of them were on their own adventure. Key West seemed to have an ever-changing group of bums.

My adventure of the road was drawing to a close, though. After awhile, an adventure stops being an adventure and becomes part of life. It's exciting when everything you do is new and different. The views are more spectacular and the colors more vibrant when the adventure is beginning. But in time, what you do to survive becomes routine, and the edge comes off. After I had been gone for a year, I went home. One of the first things my dad did was to ask me what I was planning to do. He said, "Being on the road starts becoming a habit." He was right. At some point, it becomes the only thing that you know. I was proud of him for making an effort to communicate.

After Key West, we started up the east coast of Florida. There are a lot more beaches to hang out on there. Our days of hanging out on the beach were just that. We would park the van somewhere near the beach, and we would just occupy time by reading, or we might go swimming. Sometimes, I would go for a run on the beach. I was still close enough to my cross-country and track days to enjoy just running along and feeling the warm breezes and the sensation of my body breathing heavily. The beaches ran on forever, and there wasn't anything to stop me except my unwillingness to go any farther.

We got to Daytona right about spring break time for a lot of college students. Daytona was the only beach I remember being at where you drove your vehicle right out on the beach. Even though it was the wildest environment a lot of these normally studious young people had ever been in, I felt it was just more of the same. Don't get me wrong; I was having fun, but it was not the sort of time that left an indelible mark on my memory. Fact is, I don't remember many details of that time. I think that's because I was looking for that sense of adventure and wonder that I used to feel back in the beginning. It was taking more and more to make me feel like I was having the time of my life. I probably hadn't found the right party. Come to think of it, I wasn't with Joe that night, and that meant that he hadn't led me to that party that I was looking for. Maybe I was getting used to that ability of his to find a party.

The truth is, I don't think I had the kind of personality that attracted parties. I'm not sure what intangible characteristic made people want to invite you to a party. I think it's an aura. Joe had an aura about him with his engaging conversation and slight smile that made people trust him. When you talked to Joe, there was something that told you that no matter what happened, you were going to have a good time.

The days began to run together, and the time seemed to be nothing special. The only thing that I remember was my growing dissatisfaction with the situation and my desire to find a nice place to be with someone that I felt close to. Of course, I'm referring to someone that could give me more satisfaction than I was getting with Joe. I'm sure most of you know what I'm saying.

Eventually, we made our way up to Birmingham. Joe wanted to go to Colorado, and Robin's mother's house was on the way in Birmingham. Robin's mom was glad to see her and had a normal house, but it seemed so weird to have a mother who was okay to have her fifteen-year-old daughter out hitchhiking on the road and going to Mardi Gras when everyone else's fifteen-year-old daughter was in school at that time of the year. It didn't fit into my preconceptions of motherhood.

While we were in Birmingham, I told Joe that I was going to go back to New Orleans. I didn't tell him it was because I was having trouble mentally with all the stealing. That wasn't all of it. I had been thinking that I was ready for something different for awhile. Since leaving Key West the first time, I had been thinking about finding a place that I could stay for awhile with a woman and see what a more established existence was like. I was getting a bad feeling that somewhere along the line something had to go wrong, and I was afraid of the consequences. The fact that we had gone as far as we had in a stolen van was amazing. I figured that all it would take would be to get caught stealing ten dollars at some gas station that was sitting out and then somebody would find out the van was stolen, and then "hello, prison" for everybody. As it turned out, the van did get confiscated by the police in Colorado, and everybody got away free, but that's another story. Joe wanted me to stay with them because actually we were closer to each other than the others were. In about three weeks, we had seen and done a bunch. Even though now I don't like a thief, I wouldn't trade my time in the van for anything.

At three o'clock in the morning, the van dropped me off on I-59, and we said good-bye, even though it wasn't the last time we saw each other. After they had been arrested in Colorado and let go for lack of evidence, they all came back to the apartment in New Orleans.

So there I was on the interstate thumbing my way toward New Orleans and the kind of life that I wanted to try. Even though there were practically no cars on the highway, the first car to come down the pike was an old early '60s Plymouth station wagon. It stopped and picked me up. I think it was destiny for me to go back. The guy was going all the way to New Orleans, and he had some killer pot. He gave me a couple of different bags and asked me to roll a couple of joints. I did it with pride, of course. We rode and smoked and talked for a couple of hours. After awhile, I got pretty sleepy, and he said that I should just crawl in the back and crash if I wanted too. I did. He woke me up when he was on Esplanade Avenue and dropped me off a block from the apartment. It was a beautiful spring morning as I walked to it. As I walked in the front door leading to the stairs to the second-story apartment, Jonnie came to the top of the stairs. I don't believe she has ever been as glad to see me as she was that day. She had hoped I was coming back but didn't really think I was.

The simple act of walking through that door changed my life and pointed me in a new direction. Jonnie and I lived together in New Orleans and Colorado for a year before we got married because she was pregnant. We had a son and later had two girls. We are still married thirty-five years later. We both went to college, got degrees, and became teachers. I figured all through our marriage that we were destined to be together, because how many couples do you know that have been living together since the first day they met? Except, of course, for that two-week period in Florida.

EPILOGUE TWO

Now I have written my story. I guess it wasn't a fantastic story. I guess this story is not going to change anyone's life, but it sure changed mine. At least now my kids will have my story before I get too old and senile to remember it. Do you think they will like reading about my sex life—or lack of?

You will notice that the title to this chapter is "Epilogue Two." My first attempt at an epilogue started out with me quoting some statistics about the population doubling in forty years and that somewhere down the road there has to be a catastrophe that kills off a large portion of the population. I was also going into a tirade about how our society is on a downhill slide, but that is not what this story is about. Yes, I am worried about this country and about the world, but all I can do is live with the cards that are dealt to me. This country has changed a lot in thirty-five years and is going to change even more in the next thirty-five years, but we can't worry about that. We are doomed to keep living our lives until we can't anymore.

If someone were to ask me if I recommended that everyone have an adventure, I would say yes. I don't think it is a terrible idea that all students be required to have a year-long adventure before they go to college. Actually, if a congressman were passing a law stating that nobody could go to college before they had a year-long adventure, I would fight it, because I wouldn't want my kids to go through what I did. The way things are now, I would lock my kids in the basement before I let them go hitchhiking around the country for a year. But since I don't have a basement, it's not going to come to that.

It has been two years since I spent the summer laying out this story. Since then, my wife of thirty-six or thirty-seven years died. It was thirty-seven if you count how many years we lived together. We lived together from the first day we met. Because of that, I often felt that we were meant to be together. When the marriage got bad at times, I never felt it should, or could die.

In the year after we started living together, we lived for six months in Leadville, Colorado, which is the highest-elevation city in the United States. Jonnie was born and spent her whole life below sea level in New Orleans. When we were first in Leadville, we used to have to walk about six blocks uphill to the grocery store at ten thousand feet. I thought she was going to die by the time we got to the store. Luckily, it was downhill going back home with the groceries.

Well, anyway, by the time we left Colorado, she was pregnant. Teenagers just don't believe that anything is going to come back and bite them in the ass later on. Just like when they start smoking for the dumbest reasons, they don't believe or don't think that they will have to suffer the consequences. So when we had sex, we took no precautions such as using prophylactics or any other contraceptives, because we were too involved in the moment. Anyway, when we got back to New Orleans, we got married when she was four months pregnant. This accounts for my discrepancy as to whether she was my wife for thirty-six or thirty-seven years.

When we got married at a justice of the peace one Friday night after work, she was beginning to show. The justice of the peace started the ceremony with, "Sir, I'm about to do you a great disservice." That comment did not make Jonnie happy. We had our two best friends as witnesses, and at the last minute, her dad showed up with her little brother and sister. I don't believe she ever loved her dad more than she did at that moment.

In those days, living together or getting married when you were pregnant was looked down upon by upstanding citizens of society. My older brother and sister and her older brother and sister all got married after a proper courtship at churches with the whole nine yards of ceremony. They started living together *after* their marriages. If you would have polled both our families of our chances of surviving, I doubt anybody would have given us five years.

After the wedding, we went out with our friends for a little while and went back to our roach-infested dump for the night. I had no real skills in the job market and was making $2.25 an hour as a carpenter's helper. I brought home a whopping $70-80 a week. We were barely paying the $120 rent and were living on about thirty dollars a week for expenses. One time, I decided to put ten dollars away somewhere in our apartment for the next week but forgot where I hid it. She would still bring that up thirty-five years later. The future did not look bright.

In the early years of marriage, Jonnie was, as the expression goes, full of piss and vinegar. She didn't like anyone to tell her to do anything. She hated having anyone tell her she couldn't do something. When I told her, "Stop sweeping the kitchen trash onto the back porch. Pick up your own trash." She said, "Okay." She then continued to sweep the kitchen trash onto the porch.

Less than a month after having our third child, she went to the local college and enrolled. She's the only person I know that dropped out of high school, got her GED, and graduated from college. It took her ten years to graduate. She convinced me to enroll in college so that I could help her with her math. Then, the first time we took a math class together, she was too stubborn to listen to me. I don't think I would have graduated from college, if it weren't for her.

The best thing she ever did for herself was to become a teacher. She was a very good teacher. I never met one of her former students who didn't think the world of her. Both my daughters had her as a teacher. She was constantly teaching them. She was always asking them, "What kind of clouds are those?" or "What kind of rock formations are those?"

All my kids grew up with a strong scientific background. My son now teaches science.

About ten years ago, a broken leg and a bout of pneumonia helped her weight to balloon up over four hundred pounds. She was always overweight. From the time our third kid was born till she broke her leg, her weight was over three hundred. When her weight got up over four hundred, combined with her smoking, her health started to get real bad. I began to pull away emotionally from her, because I didn't feel she was going to last long. It wasn't intentional. It just happened.

Jonnie finally got a gastric bypass, which is where they sew off half of the stomach and reattach the intestines to the top half of it. A lot of people who are not overweight look at a person that is and think, *All they have to do is lose the weight.* It is not that easy. If you're overweight and you do decide that it's time to lose two hundred pounds, you can be extremely good at sticking to it for a week or even a month and lose fifty or seventy-five pounds, but sooner or later, you are going to think you deserve to have a day off. Naturally, as you will go back on the diet, you begin to think you can go off the diet again and still get back on it. Except each time you get back on, it's for shorter and shorter timeframes. Every time you go off the diet, it becomes easier next time. After a while, you tend to go off it for good. Two hundred pounds is just too hard to lose. You have to change the way you think and live to be successful. Having the operation forces you to not have a day off. The consequences of taking a day off are pain and nausea.

Jonnie lost two hundred pounds in a short amount of time, but she didn't stick to the change of thinking that goes with the operation. She didn't maintain a healthy diet. She didn't maintain an exercise routine. She would go through spells where 75 percent of what she ate was Cheez-Its, or pretzels, or crackers. The lack of good nutrition took its toll. About five years ago, she wanted to take a trip to the Grand Canyon because she didn't think she was going to live much longer. Even though I didn't think we could afford it, I agreed, because I had been thinking the same thing. That attitude governed the last five years of her life. She didn't care if whatever she wanted was going to affect my finances long after she died; she wanted what she wanted right then, because she was going to die early. Most of my ancestors lived into their eighties and nineties. I needed to think about retirement, and she never let me. I was weak.

In the end, all she thought about was pain. Her stomach hurt, or her knee hurt. She had her knee replaced less than a year before her death. She was very creative in her description of her pain. She said that the pain in her stomach was like knotted-up snakes. I'm not sure how much of her pain was from fibromyalgia, her imagination, vitamin deficiencies, or a dependence on Oxycodon, but it consumed her life. She talked about getting on medical disability and retiring, but we both knew she would not last long like that. When she wasn't working, she did nothing. She did very little housework, did nothing outside, and didn't want to go anywhere. Teaching is the only thing that kept her alive for the last few years.

She spent most, if not all, her time in the front of the house that used to be the garage. We didn't spend a lot of our time together, mostly because she spent most of her time with a lit cigarette. She was a sloppy smoker to boot. The tabletops had a heavy layer of trash, ashes, and cigarette butts. All her ashtrays were piled high with butts. There were cigarette-burn spots on the floor, the couch, and all her nightclothes from her dropping her lit cigarette when she fell asleep. I had often imagined myself walking into that part of the house and finding her dead.

So one Saturday afternoon about 3:00, my daughter and I walked into the front room after watching a movie in the living room. I went to the bathroom for a minute while my daughter went to the large tub that Jonnie spent a lot of time in. She then yelled that something was wrong. When I went in, there was no water in the tub, and Jonnie was unnaturally bent over forward. As I got in the tub, I felt that her back was cold, but when I sat her up, her front was still warm, and her lips were blue. Without going into any more details, we called for an ambulance, and they pronounced her dead.

Wasn't that depressing? Here I am trying to entertain you, and I go into that depressing story. Let's have a little vote. All those out there that have quit reading this book because of the last two pages, raise your hand. Everybody look around. How many people do you see with their hands up? That's just as I thought. How about you? Are any of you out there surprised by what you see? I know! Me too! Now, concentrate, we have to trudge on through so we can get to the end of this book. We know that you cannot claim to your friends and acquaintances that this is one of the books you've read unless we push on through to the last page. Wait! I'll bet there are some people out there who are not reading this, yet will claim to have read the book. How negative of me. Anyway, the last bit of communication we had went like this:

"Where did that ten-dollar bill go that was on the table?" asked Alice, my middle child, who also has her own complete set of problems.

"I haven't seen it today," I quickly quipped, knowing that it had been on the table for several days, but not that day.

"I didn't take it," Jonnie insisted. I was beginning to think that she went on the defensive pretty damn quick. She then added, "Ali, Aallii! You know I wouldn't do that. You know I wouldn't take your ten dollars!"

We both knew she would if it meant vodka or cigarettes; however, we also knew she hadn't been out of the house in two days, which tended to back up her story. I also noted a little glint in her eye that I hadn't seen often lately, and the faintest trace of a smile. I then felt maybe I could add a little clarity to the conversation by laying out a little response-oriented comment.

"I don't know. She seems to be too quick to deny responsibility."

Alice said reassuringly, "It's okay, Mom. I know you didn't take it."

"See! At least my daughter believes me," she replied with a full-fledged smile. She then mischievously flipped me the bird. You know what I'm talking about. She stuck up her middle finger and pointed at me.

"I'm going to take a bath," she said as she toddled off toward the front room with her drink in her hand, and we went to watch a movie. I can't think of a more appropriate last bit of communication between her and I. It sort of summed up everything.

Here I am, more than thirty-five years later, in the same position as I was before this started. I have not had sex in eleven months. For the last five years of her life, I didn't have sex more than a half a dozen times. I have no girlfriend. I've tried bars, but when you are over fifty-five and you sit in a bar, most of the girls are my kids' ages, and the competition is stacked against me. I would have to lay down some pretty clever conversation to beat out the other nine guys vying for a girl's attention. If I recollect, I already told you that I wasn't that good at being invited to parties. I don't have much confidence in my ability to "lay down some rap," as we used to say. If you do run into an unattached woman my age at a bar, she usually looks like she's been run over by life. It goes back to that Groucho Marx opinion of women. If I got a woman that wanted to go home with me, I'd say, "What's wrong with her?"

The truth is that I have a penance to pay, in the form of, "Be careful what you wish for." More than once in the last five years of Jonnie's life, I wished that if she was going to die, that she would die before I was too old to be able to find someone else. Every year, as I got older and my body began to wear out and my level of desire grew weaker, I wanted some passion in my life and wondered if I was going to be able to deliver it. I didn't want to be looking for women in my sixties. Notice I said *women*. I wasn't interested in finding one more woman. Since I had only been with three women, I wanted to have multiple relationships. I always thought that I could be good at sex. Right now, I'm thinking that won't happen. I will never find out.

Since that's not going to be a very good ending to the book, could you hold on a minute? There's somebody at the door.

Time passes.

Oh, would you excuse me? Jane, a beautiful woman about my age that I met at the store recently, was at the door with three of her friends.

They had just realized that they needed a physical release because they felt that it would relieve the stress imposed on them from society. They felt that I was the best person to help them in achieving that result. I gotta go.

The daydream strikes again.

THE RISE AND FALL
OF A DICTATOR

I used to work at a paint manufacturer when I was young. Actually, I worked for two different paint manufacturers. There is a point when making paint where you mix the thick, gooey resin with the pigments with a high-speed mixer in a tank so that you can theoretically get the pigment completely saturated in the resin. It's called the grind stage. It's sort of like mixing flour into a cake mix. The better it's mixed in, the better the product. The friction from mixing at high speed heats the mixture up until a foggy, solvent cloud starts coming out in wisps from the top of the tank. The cloud could look pretty evil. It tended to look like a witch's brew.

People thought I was pretty crazy around there. One time, Milton and I were playing a pretty good trick on Wally. I had taken the forklift up to the front warehouse, turned off the propane bottle that served as the fuel, and walked back to our work area.

"What did you do with the forklift?" Walter asked.

"I left it in the front warehouse," I replied.

"Why did you leave it up there?" Walt sure was in a questioning mood, don't you think?

"I don't know. I just didn't feel like bringing it back." I gave him my best "I don't give a shit" look and pretended to be working. He went toward the front warehouse with a disgusted look, shaking his head slowly like he was tired of working with stupid white people. As he got out of sight, I told Milton what I had done.

A few minutes later, Wally's lanky six-foot-eight body returned to the work area, and he was not happy. "Now I know why you left it there. You didn't want to have to change out the bottle." Our forklifts had been converted to propane because it was cheaper and less flammable. When the forklifts ran out of fuel, you had to unhook the bottle, take it out back by the propane tank, pick up a replacement, take it back, and hook it back up. Needless to say, anytime you could, you would try to get somebody else stuck with doing all that instead. Since Wally had gotten on the forklift, started it, and gone twenty feet before it ran out of gas, he assumed I'd left it for someone else to fill.

"So what?" I calmly, nonchalantly remarked. By now, Milton was heading up front to retrieve the forklift.

"I'm not replacing the bottle. It ran out on you, so you have to replace it," he said with a strong undertone of being pissed off.

"I don't feel like doing it." I stressed the word *feel,* which indicated that I thought I was too good to do any common duties associated with the job. I was the only white guy working in back for the paint company. I quite often had to play head games with the others to keep them from running their head games on me. Call it working-man politics in the workplace.

"So, either go replace it yourself or not. I'm not doing it." Wally's eyes were glowing a nice shade of red. I always loved Wally's eyes when they had that red glow.

Right about then, Milton came roaring by in the forklift. The timing was perfect. You know how sometimes you set up a practical joke on somebody, and the timing just doesn't quite work? Well, that wasn't this time. Considering that it was a spur-of-the-minute joke, it went well. Wally's expression was priceless. His jaw dropped as he looked at Milton, and I laughed at him hysterically.

Whenever I work around somebody for a while, I tend to pick up their expressions and mannerisms. More than once over the years, my wife would stop me and ask who used the expression I was using at that moment. At that time, since I worked around a bunch of blacks, I didn't just laugh at something like that, I got hysterical, complete with spastic body convulsions and had to lean up against something for support. It was the mannerism of the people I worked around, and as I said earlier, I copy other people's mannerisms.

As I was in the midst of my well-acted convulsions, I noticed one of the guys that worked up in shipping was walking by, and he gave me a very strange look. As I said, most of the people that worked around me thought I was mental. Most of them thought I had been sniffing too much solvent. There were only two solvents around there that would give you a buzz. One was methylene chloride, and the other was toluol. Most of the time, I avoided getting any sort of a buzz from inhaling solvents. I always thought it was the high of the desperate, like teenagers. The airplane glue of my youth handed out its buzz from toluol. Most of the time, you ended up with a headache.

So there was Samuel, giving me a strange look as I happened to be drumming off a tank of epoxy. We had just thinned it down after getting it pretty hot in the grind stage. As I was pouring it into drums, the solvent was still coming off the mixture in wispy little clouds. Anyway, as I was laughing hysterically at Wally, Samuel was looking at me like I was high from solvent. Without skipping a beat, I looked at Samuel and yelled, "Hey, come on over here and smell this. It's great." I put my head down by the hot paint, took a big huff of cloud, and then continued laughing hysterically. Now, if Samuel would have come over and smelled that batch of epoxy, all he would have gotten was nauseous. The most prominent solvent in that concoction was MEK, which is the only solvent I know that you can taste as you smell it, and it is bitter. If I had done that a couple of years earlier, I probably would have puked, but since I had gotten somewhat used to the smell, I could huff on that crap for the sake of the joke and not get sick. Samuel walked away with his eyes big, shaking his head. It's not often that you get two good jokes out of one situation.

So anyway, I decided to write a fun piece of poetry about the establishment where I worked, on the bathroom wall above the urinal, of course. The title of this unique work of art was the same as the name of the company. It went:

Industrial Coatings
Bubble, bubble,
Toil and trouble.
Wing of a bat, eye of a toad.
You don't like the way I do it,
Hit the road!

I thought it was extremely clever, but I don't think anybody else really appreciated it. Nobody made any comments. It might have been because most of the guys around there couldn't read.

It took me ten years of teaching before I felt like I was getting good at it. I felt I was always pretty good at breaking down the material into understandable bites for the students. But I was not very good at getting the students to do what they were supposed to do. Discipline was the hardest for me to be good at. I had to test out a hundred tricks over the years to find out what worked and what didn't. Sometimes a trick that works on one kid won't work on another.

After I had been teaching for a few years, my wife said that I had become much more confrontational. One of the things the paint job had taught me was that it didn't pay to piss off everyone around you. After awhile, one of the people you have pissed off will find a way to get even. In fact, that's how I got fired from that job. So before I became a teacher, I was all about being low drag. "Do not rock the boat" was my motto. However, when dealing with teenagers, you have to be willing to get right up in their faces to make sure they know when you are upset.

I went to the local commuter university for secondary math education. That gave me lots of electives, because I didn't have a minor. I took algebra, linear algebra, thirteen hours of calculus, and the kicker was differential equations, which did nothing for me in an effort to teach geometry to a high school student that hates math. I learned way more math in college to become a high school math teacher than I needed to know. I am overqualified in math to teach it.

I took about fifteen hours of psychology, which definitely helps me have an insight into the things teenagers think. I had maybe fifteen hours of courses in teaching methods, which helps but does not spell out exactly how you get thirty kids at a time do what you want them to. The reason they don't tell you exactly how to get thirty kids to do what you want them to do is because everyone has to find his or her own method. It is retarded for a young teacher to try and control a class using my methods. Yes, I know that it is not politically correct to refer to anything using the word *retarded*, but it's a word I grew up with. When someone does something that makes no sense, *retarded* is the word that feels right. I figure it's not really a derogatory remark toward people what are mentally handicapped, because they're not called retarded anymore. Last year's students learned the word *asinine* and decided it was a good descriptor. After all, assholes love doing asinine things.

Anyway, over the years, I've learned a few tricks toward getting kids to do what I've wanted them to do. One of the best tricks is the look. The look has to be practiced and perfected. I prefer to clear my mind and face of all emotion. I look at the student for as long as I can. I want the silence and look to get as uncomfortable as possible. Kids are a good place to practice the look on. Most teenagers hate to be stared at. If you get good at it, it is a good way to convey your thoughts on everyone, not just teenagers.

My story, though, is about the principal that went away. The district school board has always been ashamed of my school. That's why they sent a committee to investigate why we always had the lowest scores. It was called an ACT or DAT team, or something else with three letters.

When it came down to the housecleaning that this little team wanted the principal to do, the principal at the time said no, so they had to find another principal.

I walked away from the SPAT team with a wonderful reputation, because I ran into the craziest curriculum specialist in the central office named Barry. A lot of people considered Barry a flake. He walked into my worst class one morning with the intentions of observing. My classes tend to be less structured than other classes at times, because learning can be accelerated in those unstructured situations, but the risk is that the teacher sometimes can let it get out of hand.

This class, on the other hand, was not one that I let get away with anything. Sometimes you just get an odd mixture of young males of varied ethnic backgrounds who tend to just piss you off all the time. I was always verbally harassing these guys. All it takes is three or more guys in a room who are looking for attention to ruin a class. If you throw a few part-time dickheads and do-nothings into the mixture, you have the makings of a miserable class. Well, that was this class.

I let the class have thirty minutes to do a study guide for a test the next day. Little Robbie, who was the current number-one white dickhead in the school, asked, "Do we get a cheat sheet for tomorrow?"

I tilted my head like I was thinking for effect and replied, "That's a big, definite maybe. Depends on how much you get done in this class today."

As I sat down and let them get started, Barry asked me about the cheat sheet. I told him that it was just a method of getting them to focus on what they need to know for the test. There are two basic sizes I allow them to have. There's the standard 1½ x 1½ inch and the 1 x 1 inch for when a class ticks me off.

"They have to be small because it helps create the image of really cheating, which helps them to really get involved. When they are forced to decide just what information they need the most so that they can put it on their small cheat sheet, they get a better idea of what they do know,"

I explained. Barry thought that was great. It was a real "thinking out of the box" example.

Now, since I had been verbally harassing this group so much, a bunch of them had started getting a little bonding thing going on. Sometimes the ones who get yelled a lot at home tend to get attached to teachers that yell at them a lot. That's me. Didn't I tell you I was verbally harassing them? That translates into yelling. Anyway, since I had this strange person who was obviously from the central office in my classroom asking questions, they figured they should act like good, interested students. They decided that they wanted to make me look good. They came up, asked questions, and then went back to their chairs and worked together with others. Don't be surprised. The ones that know how to disrupt the class the most know exactly what it takes to be a good student. They just choose to act like asses.

When thirty minutes was up, I told them to get quiet, and I only had to use a little of my serious voice to get it to happen. I did not start going over the study guide until they were quiet and paying attention. It went exactly how a class is supposed to go. I still gave them only a one-by-one-inch cheat sheet out of general principle. If I hadn't had Barry from the central office, it is unlikely that I would have gotten such a favorable review.

Education has its own variation of the Peter's Principal. The Peter's Principal is the idea that a man will rise to his own ineptitude. You know, where if a guy is the hardest worker on the crew, then the company will give him a promotion to foreman. However, just because a guy is the hardest worker doesn't necessarily mean that he'll be the best foreman. A different set of skills is needed when you're trying to get others to do what you want them to. Every time you do the job right, they're going to give you another promotion until you find the job that's too tough for you. Therefore, everyone rises to the level of their incompetence.

With education, it goes, "If you can't hold down a job doing anything else, you become a teacher. If you can't teach, you administrate." I'm sure there is a large percentage of administrators that are administrators because they just didn't like being in the classroom. Being a teacher is not for everybody. In case you haven't heard this from me, it's not easy getting thirty teenagers to do what you want them to. Many teachers never do get thirty teenagers to do what they want them to, and for many of them, they choose to go into administration.

I believe that the reason we got stuck with Denise, our new principal, was that the old principal of the big high school just up the road decided he didn't want her as an assistant principal anymore. I had heard that she had an affair with one of the teachers at Big Daddy High. Take that with a grain of salt. Just because I heard that doesn't make it true. I will say this: knowing what I know about her, I would not be surprised if it were true. Mr. Buck, who was the principal at Big Daddy High, was principal there for close to thirty years. He had plenty of friends in the central office. If he had an assistant principal that he didn't want around anymore, the easiest way of getting rid of that person was to get him or her promoted out. I believe that is a common method also used in government jobs.

Denise's job was to get rid of some people that the SQUAT team had recommended be gone. Remember, I wasn't on that list. The first time I met Denise, she told me that she had heard that I was a good teacher. This was the first I'd heard that the central office was giving out good reports about me. Who else in the central office thought I was good, besides Barry? With the twenty-twenty hindsight that I have collected over the years, I look back and realize that she didn't really want to get on my bad side. Not that I'm so fearsome. It was a matter of me having a lot to do with the central office's method of grading her. How students do on the state exit examination (SEE) made a large percentage of the formula for grading schools by the state. Since the tenth graders took their math part of the test that year, I was their last chance to learn what they hadn't learned up until then. Without my knowledge, I was important to her.

My previous stint in the "real world" had taught me a few tricks on how to deal with bosses. Denise didn't have the work experience that

I had had. She didn't work for Industrial Coatings, Crazy Charlie, or Weird Wayne. Government workers, like teachers or school employees, are somewhat sheltered in their jobs. It's not easy getting rid of bad government employees. Teachers have tenure. If a teacher makes it three years without doing anything stupid and keeps his or her job, then he or she has tenure. After that, it takes a lot of paperwork to get rid of a bad teacher. Do you have any idea how bad I would have to be to get fired as a math teacher? That's why I offer all my students bonus points for getting me fired. I sincerely believe that this is the biggest factor in why I have had so few complaints by parents. The students are reluctant to give a teacher what they ask for. Every time I offer the points, somebody always asks how I would give out bonus points if I got fired. Sometimes they surprise you by not being as dumb as they look.

Commercial jobs, on the other hand, want you to prove you deserve to keep your job. A boss in the real world, as we like to say in education, can tell you at anytime that you are no longer employed. The trick to keeping a job at a commercial establishment is to make yourself more valuable there than at someplace down the road. It involves some politics in the form of sucking up when it's convenient and showing some attitude at times. Attitude is important. You can't let them take you for granted. At the boatyard, for example, I always came in when I felt like it. I had already proven that I did good work. I worked long hours when needed, and I could figure some stuff out. I had figured a few things out that nobody else did. It's a good thing, too, because I am slow. The coming-in-late thing was mainly just to show that I could have an attitude if need be.

Never let your employer think you are perfect. As soon as they think you're going to do everything they ask you to do, and that you're going to do a fantastic job, they start getting unrealistic expectations of you. Sometimes you need to tell them no, you're not going to do that, or that the project is going to fail. It makes it easier on you if they don't think you're perfect.

The reason all that extra experience has come in handy is because I knew principals have very little authority when it comes to firing teachers. Every time I do something wrong in school, I have to ask the same questions: Am I going to get fired? Will I lose any money? Will I go to jail?

I actually have to ask that last one more than the other two. With teaching, even though I said it was hard to get fired, there is a whole list of things that will get you fired in a hurry, and many of them are illegal. If a girl tells her parents and administrators that you sexually molested her, then they will consider you guilty until you can prove otherwise. Teenage girls are hard to read sometimes. They can mistake a little attention that you give them as an invitation for more. Too many times, they don't know what they want, and you may be what they think they want. So far, nothing like that has happened to me, even though I probably tend to dance too close to the line of what's acceptable. I am told repeatedly not to touch the kids, but I still will give them a little hug, although it's always up around the shoulder.

I never let Denise think that she had anything on me. I let her have some attitude from the beginning. Three new math teachers were hired the year she came in. She had been very active in taking over the new school. Two of the new math teachers were black.

The white teacher was a bit political. There are plenty of good teachers who come in and do the best they can for the students and aren't looking for any attention for doing their job. Then there are teachers who are always looking for some recognition in any way they can. Sandy was like that. Years later, she became part of the curriculum committee that was determining how the teachers were going to teach their subjects. It was a good idea that if everyone was on the same page, then a student could change teachers for any reason and not have too hard a time catching up. The problem with that, for me, was that I had been doing this for more than ten years and knew more geometry than anyone I knew. I had not just learned geometry out of a book or at college. I learned geometry by building piers on the river, offshore housing, ductwork, houses, and boats. I have a broad resume in carpentry. The geometry needed when building a boat would blow most students' minds. The activities the curriculum committee recommended were not as good as mine. You're right, that does sound conceited. So what? The curriculum committee would have had a better product if they would have just taken my worksheets and used them.

One time, we were having a tutoring session after school for the SEE. It was the first year the state was making the tenth graders take the SEE, so they gave every school some extra money for tutoring. Luther was an overweight special education student with fairly bright red hair. He was in there and said something toward me that was derogatory, or maybe it just irritated me. I immediately went to the high moral ground and said, "Luther, you're a moron." You can easily see how I could have gone with something childish and immature. "No, wait a minute. You're a stupid moron." That helped clarify my feelings, but it wasn't quite there yet, so I added, "No, wait a minute. You're a stupid, ugly moron, and if your mom liked you, she'd dress you funny." The other teachers there all had their mouths open in disbelief that I had said that to a student.

Very little of what I told Luther hurt his feelings. I was a little irritated with Luther that day. He was taking my class for the second time and hadn't turned in all the projects. Luther wasn't stupid, but he was lazy. Many special ed. students get an attitude that even if they don't do everything they're supposed to, they should still be given a passing grade. They get this attitude legitimately, because a lot of teachers feel like special ed. students are just not capable of handling the work, and they do give them passing grades for inferior work. I don't care if you think you're bad at math or not; if you want to pass my class, you at least have to try. Not handing in assignments was like not making an effort, and I don't like lack of effort.

Luther had also been part of the wrestling team for the last two years. The previous year, he had been competing at tournaments. That particular year, he was too old to compete, but he still participated in practice. I knew that Luther was not going to go home to his parents and try to get me in trouble, because I knew Luther's dad, and I knew that plumber wouldn't object. I also knew that Luther's mom had gotten a new boyfriend that year and kicked Luther out of the house to live with his dad. His dad did not live in our district. The only way for Luther to go to the school he was used to was to not tell anyone and get a ride home. I was the one that gave Luther a ride home. So you see, I knew I wasn't going to get into any trouble from Luther or his family, because they knew I was trying. The only thing that I had said that might have hurt him was, "If your mom liked you ..."

About fifteen minutes after I had commented to Luther, Denise came fluttering through the classroom. I say *fluttered* because most of the time, that's what she did. I would say she had ADD. She couldn't hold onto an idea for very long. When she first started, she wanted me to tell her jokes. I soon realized that I couldn't tell her a joke that was too long, because she couldn't focus that long. Anyway, Sandy wasted no time telling the principal, "You should have heard what he said to Luther. He told him that he was stupid and ugly." I don't know if she was playing a game of "I'll make you look bad so that I'll look better"_or not, but I didn't really care.

Just to clear out exactly what I had said, I repeated it. Denise then said, "You know, if any parents come around to complain about what you said to these kids, we won't have a leg to stand on."

"That must explain all those complaints you've gotten about me." I've only had two parents come to the school and complain about me in over twenty years. Considering the things I say and do compared to others, that is amazing.

"I haven't had any parents complain about you," she replied.

"Oh, that's right. In fact, 504 Boy's dad came down here and demanded that he be put back into my class. Didn't he? I wonder how that happened." She was confused. She knew who 504 Boy was, but she was confused as to how I could say the things I say and not get into any trouble.

A student that is classified 504 means that they have a learning disability and that we are required by law to accommodate that student in the ways that they've diagnosed. Notice I said *diagnosed*. For example, if a student has trouble focusing for long periods, their IEP might say that we should give them extra time to take a test. In the junior high that fed into our school, they had interpreted that to mean that they should give all open book, open notebook tests and generally give them the grade. It's easier to do that than be sued. When Steven got to my class, he had learned quite a bit about having an easy time in class by applying the 504 card.

One day, we were on the second day of a study guide that I had given them for a test the next day. Steven then decided to play his 504 card by telling me, "My mom looked at all the work you gave us and said that I was 504 and that was too much work for me."

"Oh, really? I'll bet you sucked up on that, didn't you? Did you tell her that you had the whole class period yesterday and the whole class period today? You like having her say that you can't, just so you won't have to. Is that what you really think of yourself? So far, you've been doing good, and as long as you are trying in my class, I'll take care of you. But if you're looking for the easy route, good luck."

After that, there were two Stevens that showed up to class, but seldom at the same time. There was one guy that came in, did his work, asked questions, and got Cs on tests. Then there's the wimpy, whiney kid who talked more than he should and just didn't get it because he wanted something easier. The latter was 504 Boy. It was a small class, and the other students would start calling him 504 Boy when he was in that particular mood. They could get away with it because they were his friends. Usually, when they started calling him 504 Boy, he would snap right out of it.

A few years back, I had told another teacher that I had grown up with that I had called one kid 504 Boy. I tend to brag a bit too much about my accomplishments. She started practically ranting at me that that was terrible and I was going to get fired. She never did hear the whole story about 504 Boy, because she was too busy telling me that I was an idiot.

At the end of the first semester, the computer had all the classes mixed up and new. I told all my students that if they wanted to have me, they had to make sure they had algebra first hour, because that was the only hour I was teaching it. Practically everyone that had me first semester, made sure they had me first hour again. Steven didn't. When the second semester came around, that class that had thirteen in it now had twenty-five. Steven was in a class that was highly structured, and it didn't suit him as well, so he came to me and asked if he could get back into my class. I told him no, because I had told him that if he wanted to be in my class, he needed to get a schedule change. I also didn't want to add another student to an already big class. A third reason was because Denise had said she didn't want students to think they could just change classes because they didn't like a teacher.

The next week, Denise came up and told me that Steven's dad had come down to the school and insisted that Steven get put back into my class. I told her that I didn't care. I'm pretty sure that the term *504* got batted around more than once in that little meeting.

I knew that Luther and his family were not going to complain about me or my comment. The next year, Luther invited me to the FFA banquet. Every year, FFA has a banquet at which seniors in the organization were allowed to invite the teacher that they thought had done the most for them to the dinner. Denise was there because she was the principal. I asked her if she knew who invited me to the banquet and then told her that it was Luther, the guy that I'd called a stupid, ugly moron. She didn't say anything, but the look was priceless. She never knew how to take me. Of course, I tried to make sure she never got me.

One of the new black teachers that Denise hired the first year was an older, battle-weary survivor of the racial prejudices of the South. She remembered being made to drink in a different water fountain, sit in the movie balcony, and have to go to a separate amusement park. She definitely carried some extra baggage and tended to find prejudice when there was none. She came to me one day during one of my classes and wanted to talk to me in the hall. The first thing she asked me was, "Why didn't you tell me that the principal had it in for me?"

I had just recently found out that Denise did, in fact, have a problem with her. I was stumbling around for an answer, being as I hadn't told her anything. She let me off the hook after I replied, "She doesn't know how to take you. You've got her totally confused."

This was the first time that it had been spelled out to me. I hadn't realized it before, but as soon as she said it, I knew it was true. After that, I never missed an opportunity to leave Denise confused.

One time, as I walked into the cafeteria to get some lunch, she saw me and asked how my classes were going at that time. It was about March, and students at that time of the year are beginning to get that end-of-the-year attitude. They start thinking that the teachers are not these strange people trying to force them to do things they don't want to do. They start to become more familiar with the teacher and quite often look at them as almost parental figures. That feeling tends to make them feel like doing the same things in class that they do at home. They start giving the same resistance to me that they give at home. Teenagers have to give resistance to authority figures, because that is their method of breaking the emotional bonds that may keep them from becoming their own independent personages. Anyway, I sort of summed all those feelings by stating, "Oh, all right, I guess. You know, at this time of the year, you have to yell at them and call them names more."

"Oh, I don't think I want to hear about this," she said. Remember, she didn't know how to take me. I don't know if she really thought I was telling the truth or not.

I felt like I hadn't really made my feelings clear, so I added, "You know, at some point, MF just doesn't cut it anymore." I really didn't go around calling my students "little motherfuckers," but I still had to keep her wondering.

Denise was going around doing the job that she'd been assigned. She was given the job as principal to get rid of dead weight. She did her best to make the job of teaching miserable to some. There were three teachers there that she had known as children. Since two of them were on the list to get rid of, she took a sort of joy in making their lives miserable. The first thing she did was put Jack, who was a true PE teacher, into the classroom. He was certified to teach social studies, like a lot of coaches, but he hadn't coached in a few years and was definitely used to sitting around all day. He was used to watching students walk around the gym, play volleyball, or play basketball. PE teachers hate the classroom. PE jobs are normally reserved for the head football coach or some other coach.

PE jobs don't have the same crap that other teaching jobs have. Their lesson plans are like one sentence: play basketball. They don't have to grade papers, and grades are just a matter of keeping track of who dressed out that day.

The other teacher that she was gunning for was Bob. Bob was tired of teaching and getting worse every year. He was basically a miserable son of a bitch at the end. He disliked her so much that I guess you could call it hate. He was extremely pissed when she got rid of him as girls' basketball coach and gave the job to Lisa. After that, he commenced complaining nonstop when it came to Denise. She never did get rid of him, though.

Her techniques would not have had an effect on me, because I had worked for Crazy Charley and Weird Wayne. One of the new changes that she insisted on was that we should all spend the entire period on our feet. We should not just sit at our desk and try to teach. I can somewhat agree with that. Too many times, we tend to put out less effort showing and teaching so that we can spend more time sitting at our desks. However, I did not feel that I had to spend all my time walking around trying to make students learn just to please her. One day, I had shown everyone how to do the lesson and had made my rounds to make sure everyone was on the right track. I was then sitting at my desk while the students were doing their worksheets. I had music playing on the computer. I prefer the music of the late sixties and early seventies. I feel that having the younger generation listen to music other than rap is a learning experience. Most of the kids like hearing music, even if it is oldies, while they work.

Denise walked into my room at that moment. I knew that if I jumped up and acted like I had been caught doing something wrong, she would see that as a sign that she had power over me. I wanted to convey the attitude that there wasn't anything she could do to me. After all, I approached any problem with administrators with the three questions. Therefore, I definitely wasn't going to jump up to make her feel better. I then looked straight at her with the thought, *Go ahead. Tell me exactly what you want to say,* clearly in the front of my mind. I wanted to see what she was going to say. She looked at me, and I could tell she was turning over in her mind whether she should make a joke or turn it all serious by making an issue out of it. She chose to make a joke out of it. She was mine.

I wasn't playing by her rules. She was a bit of a bully. She loved having the upper hand. She tried her best to develop that upper hand with intimidation. There was a teacher named Tom that was the nervous type. The students described him as shell-shocked. They would arrange at a certain point in the class to drop their books on the floor in succession so that it would sound like mortars going off. At that point, he would practically dive under the desk. I don't know if he was in Vietnam or not, but I do know that he was easily upset. Denise picked up on that and used it to her advantage. Tom had not gotten paid for some tutoring he had done, so he called the payroll department. They told him that it was the school's job to pay that. They then called Denise and told her that it was her job to pay that. She immediately proceeded to go to his classroom and berate him in front of his class. She made sure to tell him that he was not supposed to go over her head. I can't even imagine her doing that to me.

In the first year of her reign, our SEE scores were not good. About thirty students had failed the test. Only about three of them were mine. Our scores were the worst in the district by far. This was not good for her, and since I had only three failures, she felt she had even less control through intimidation over me.

Every few years, the state board would try to find a new way of improving the failure rate of algebra students. The national average is that 40 percent of all algebra students fail. French psychologist Piaget had determined that there were stages that every child goes through in their development. At about the time that students crossed from junior high to high school, they progress from concrete operational to abstract operational. It is the time that students start to understand abstract ideas. For girls, this means that they are all about love. I can't tell you how many times I had to read "Alice loves Johnny—forever" or some such drivel on my board. Usually, by the next week, it was "Alice loves Frankie—forever."

Just because students are supposed to be able to handle abstract ideas in ninth grade does not mean that they are ready to. It's similar to when a child physically matures slower than their peers. You know, it's sort of like how I had a hairless crotch a full two years after everybody else in my class had a full bush. What seems so hard to understand when they're in ninth grade becomes so much easier in a year or two.

At that time, the state board's idea was to make an Algebra I Part One and Part Two. This gave them an extra year to catch up with abstract thinking. The problem was that a large portion of the SEE was geometry, and Algebra I Part Two didn't give them that. They weren't going to see the geometry until they were juniors. As I said, all but three of the students that failed were in the Algebra I Part Two class, and their teacher was Sandy. Political Sandy had decided to take a job at another high school in the district before the second year, which was good, in my opinion.

The second year went much better. First and most important was that we got one of those rare classes that were serious, intelligent, and well disciplined. When I was explaining something at the board, I would feel like they weren't paying attention because they were so quiet. This class was better because they were well behaved, and that meant that year after year and hour after hour, each class learned just a little bit more. It added up over the years. Because they were good classes, they were smarter. This class produced the stars in sports for four years, and the kids were good students and were quite likeable. The second part of the formula was that we'd had the worst scores in the district the previous year. We realized that the scores from the previous year were low partially because the new test had much more geometry than the previous test. Therefore, we made sure the students in Algebra I Part Two had a section of geometry.

That second year of the test, our test scores had improved drastically. We went from the bottom in the district to being in the middle of the pack. Our improvement on the scores was the best in the district. That made Denise look good in the central office. So as part of our celebration at the end of the year, the superintendant came to congratulate us on our improvement. Denise was walking down my hallway with the superintendant when they saw me. Denise told the superintendant that I was the geometry teacher and was responsible for a large share of the improvement.

He said, "Congratulations."

"I didn't have much to do with it," I lied.

"You had to have some part of it."

I figured that it was time for a joke. I know, you're not supposed to joke with the superintendent. Everyone knows that they have no sense of humor, but I went ahead and threw one out there. "I prefer to inspire the students by focusing on the reasons for trying hard. I told the students that they should look at the important aspects of doing well on the test. They should try hard, not for themselves, but so that they could make me look good. I think that's what did the trick." The superintendent laughed, and they went on their way. Denise said later that after I started to talk, she became worried about what I was going to say. She was relieved that I didn't say worse.

During the second year of her reign, I went to Grad Nite with her. Every year, as a senior trip, we, along with all the other high schools in the district, took two buses of seniors to Orlando and treated them to three days of packed-in fun. Actually, they treated us. They paid about five hundred dollars, and about eight teachers went along as chaperones.

Denise had a real thing for the young, good-looking coaches. I normally only went on Grad Nite once every four years, when I was a senior sponsor. I could only talk my wife into letting me go when I was a senior sponsor. She didn't like me having fun when she wasn't. So I had figured that I was going that year, but Denise had already decided that the starting five were going with her instead. That sort of ticked me off. It had always been an unwritten rule that senior sponsors got the choice first. I told two of the track coaches that were going as chaperones that I was a wee bit pissed. Later that night, Denise called me at home and begged me to go. I don't think it was entirely my being mad that made her call me. One of the starting five couldn't go because his wife said no. I don't think his wife liked the way Denise was acting toward her husband. Anyway, I went to Grad Nite with her.

The four days that you're together on Grad Nite are very revealing. The other chaperones were Chase, Jennifer, Lisa, Deanna, and Keith. Denise, Chase, Deanna, and Jennifer were the chaperones on one bus. Keith, Lisa, and I were on the other bus. I got lucky, I guess because I didn't want to be on the same bus as Denise. Chase and Jennifer were married, in their early twenties, and were both quite attractive. Chase was one of Denise's starting five. L. T., the basketball coach who couldn't make the trip, was one of the starters. Deanna was Elroy's wife, and Elroy, the baseball coach, was a starter. Lisa, the girls' basketball coach, was the only female starter. Rounding off the starting five was John, the football coach. I was considered the sixth man off the bench. I think that I couldn't break into the starting lineup because of my age. I was about the same age as Denise. I wasn't young enough to be a starter. Age prejudice rears its ugly head again.

Denise was always trying to mess with the starting lineup when it came to coaches. She was always firing one coach so that she could get who she wanted in his or her place. That tended to make enemies. That was the start of her downfall.

Lisa was a former student of mine. When I first started teaching, her father was on the staff. I had first hour off one year, and I was a traveling teacher, so I was usually in the lounge as my base of operations. Bryce, Jack, Roy, and Terry were all off that hour and in the lounge first hour. Jack was Lisa's dad and was a good old boy in the district. He had been around for quite a while, so he had lots of friends. Jack laid out a philosophy that hit pure gold with me. He said, "Don't do anything too good. Don't get your paperwork done right on time. If you do, they're just going to find something else to do, like some program." This is a philosophy that I live by now.

I always felt that Lisa would have had to slap my face to get me to tell her father anything negative about her. Jack was a bit hard core when it came to disciplining his two girls. He lived the old expression, "Spare the rod …" I feel that spankings or beatings should be the last resort for a parent. I feel that there are other methods of disciplining children and that parents should strive to use those other methods first. However, believe me; I definitely think that parents should whip their children when necessary. Sometimes, it is the quickest, easiest way to get your point across. The child has to understand that you will do it if needed. Whipping a child also forges an illogical bond between the two of you. It's not unusual for the child to feel that you must love them if you go to the trouble of whipping them.

Jack, on the other hand, felt that the whipping should be his first choice. There was more than one story from more than one source telling how he had a heavy hand on just about anything toward his two daughters. Lisa would never have slapped my face, though. She was, and is, a very sweet person. I personally hate using the word *sweet* when describing a person, but that is the best word to describe Lisa.

I always thought that Deanna was hot. I personally couldn't see how Elroy landed Deanna. Elroy was loud, obnoxious, and full of shit. I don't really want to go into why I felt that way. Just take my word for it, and believe that he was not good enough for her.

John didn't do Grad Nites, dances, or clubs. All John did was coach football and teach PE. Therefore, he wasn't there.

Denise was the biggest kid around once we were in the park. She always went to the most popular rides, and she wanted to ride them repeatedly. She must have hit the Rock 'n' Roller Coaster about six times in one afternoon. She was usually hyper, so she was racing to the next ride. Poor Deanna wasn't into the rides all that much, and she was getting tired of being run around. I then taught her how to set the pace from the rear. If you're constantly slowing down when traveling in a group, the group will slow down to match your pace. For a full day, she ran like crazy trying to keep up with hyper Denise and the rest of the group. She had a much better time when she could take a bit more of her time. I stayed behind with her a couple of times while the rest of the group went on some ride for the umpteenth time, and I tried to convince her to dump Elroy. I was thinking that we'd run away together. I tried to convince her that I would make her much happier. I didn't really tell her all that, but I probably should have.

On the last day, we went to the water park, Typhoon Lagoon. For some reason, there was some sort of problem with our passes, and we couldn't get into the water park. The idea behind having a successful Grad Nite is to keep the children so busy that they won't have time to get into trouble. For everyone involved, it is a distance race. I never considered having my wife go, because she couldn't keep up, and there was no place for her to go rest during the day. On the last day, the whining and complaining starts to get heavy. When we couldn't get into the water park, Denise started calling the park office to find out why and to try to figure out how to solve the problem. I was sitting on a bench when one of the other chaperones said that Denise wanted me to come sit by her so that I could handle the students that were getting rowdy. I guess she figured I knew how to settle any crap they came up with. We survived that day, and the trip.

Thus ended Denise's second year at the helm. Denise's third year was when things started to unravel for her. She started the third year in some trouble with me. She was always so impulsive. She couldn't help it. An idea would pop into her head, and there was no governing mechanism in her to think the idea through at all before she'd take off with it. It started for me when Chip, my assistant coach of the wrestling team, called to tell me that she had had our wrestling mats moved out of the closet that we had occupied for seven years. The closet was in the cafeteria, where we practiced. This happened because she happened to walk by our closet and thought that that would be a wonderful place to have a concession stand to sell candy and such. You are allowed to sell concessions during the second half of lunch, according to federal rules. My assistant coach is normally the type to think he could solve any adverse situation with his persuasive arguments. The problem is that his persuasive arguments are far too aggressive and they usually make things worse for him. Why he decided to not take the matter up personally and instead called me, I'll never know.

I got to the school about eight the next morning. Denise was not there yet. I talked to the secretary, Dana, about her move. Denise had told Dana that she had given us two portables to use for practice, so she was going to use our closet now. Dana made it sound as if she was taking a hard line toward our closet. I left a note on her door saying that we needed to talk and went over to the field house, where some other coaches were hanging out. John was there. While I was there, John got a call from the office telling him that Denise was up front and wanted to talk to him. John was her most favoritest coach on her starting five. Notice how I used the double superlative to describe John. If I had said John was her most favorite coach, it doesn't really describe the situation. When I say *most favoritest,* then you realize how favorite he was. She spent most of her time having conversations with him. She liked going to the gym during the year, finding someone to cover his class, and going to his office to tell him all of her problems. During her third year, she spent a lot of time in his office telling him all the complaints she was getting. John said, "If you ever see that woman bawling all over the place because everyone is attacking her, you won't think it's a pretty sight."

Anyway, that morning, I went back over to her office to have a talk with her. As I walked into the side door of the first hall, I could hear

Denise talking to Dana in her office. They couldn't see or hear me. "What did he say to you? Was he mad?" She sounded like she was worried about whether I was mad or not. This was to my advantage.

I walked into her office and said hello. She asked me how my summer was going. I said, "Not bad, considering you kicked me out of the closet I've had for seven years."

"I gave you two portables to use." Portables were buildings that could be moved from campus to campus as the schools got bigger. Then, when a school got a new set of classrooms, that freed up the portables to use somewhere else. Since we were the shame of the district, we were always the last ones to get new classrooms. Therefore, we always had portables around.

"We can't hold practice in a little portable for twenty guys. Somebody will get hurt." In a school argument, "someone will get hurt" is the best argument you can own. "Those mats weigh six to eight hundred pounds. I can't just move them around on a whim to find a place to practice," I added.

"Well, let's go take a look." We walked over to the cafeteria to look at the space.

"The portable only holds a third of a mat, and there are too many things in there that can hurt people if they get thrown around. We need a full mat to practice on. The only available place to hold a full mat is this cafeteria and the gym. I'm pretty sure the basketball team is not going to give up the gym. Maybe when the district decides to build us something big enough, we won't have to be stuck here. I don't see that happening anytime soon," I said, standing in the cafeteria.

"Well, I need someplace to sell concessions," she replied weakly.

Now I was ready to do some compromising. "I can give you four feet of our shelves for the candy." She didn't like it, but she realized that this was one time that she wasn't going to cram what she wanted down everyone's throat. So she said that we could move the mats back in. She didn't even take me up on the four feet of shelf space. She never sold any concessions out of our closet. That year, my assistant coach started selling concessions out of his room, and it ended up making us a lot of money. Kids always find a way to come up with money for candy, even when they don't have any money for anything else. They can find the money for a candy bar a lot easier than they can find the money for a pencil.

Her third year was the year I threatened to take her intercom away from her. As time passed in her reign, she got to feeling like the intercom was hers to use anytime she felt like it. She also started to get confused as to what her job was. Instead of taking care of her job alone, she got to thinking the school was her toy to push around any way she wanted. She got to where she felt she needed to be in the middle of everything. If two students were having an argument, she felt she needed to be the mediator. The problem was that the counselor was better equipped to do that.

The pre-dance tickets for the homecoming game were not selling well. That was typical. Students didn't want to commit to anything. They want to have their options open till the last minute. Denise decided that the seniors were not doing enough to push this dance, since it was the senior class's moneymaker. Her brilliant idea was to pick up her intercom and proceed to berate the seniors about the bad ticket sales. She went on for almost five minutes.

Normally, I would consider that all part of how schools work. The problem was that I was in the middle of class, trying to finish up the answers to a worksheet that we had been working on, and I couldn't talk over her. That evening, I went to the homecoming game early because I had to do gate duty. I was standing at the concession stand when she walked up.

"Hey, you know how everyone wants to take that marker away from John Madden during Monday Night Football because he gets carried away with it?" I asked. She didn't answer and just sort of looked at me. "Well, the next time you interrupt the middle of my class to give the seniors a hard time, I'm going to take that intercom away from you."

I said it in a joking way, but I was definitely making a statement. I was really the only one to tell her that. She was beginning to make quite a few enemies, and she didn't want anyone telling her she couldn't do something. She really wasn't listening to anyone at that point. Yet she would let me tell her something. Funny thing was, she never decided to go on a five-minute tirade in the middle of class again.

Her third year was a good year for me. That class that had done so well on the SEE the previous year were juniors now and the heart of my wrestling team. We had some cash from selling candy in our rooms, the parents were dedicated, and we were willing to travel. We started out the season thinking we were capable of being good, but the guys didn't quite believe yet. Denise didn't trust the soccer coach to take his team on an overnight trip. Yet she trusted us to go anywhere. We did four overnight tournaments. We went to a tournament in the northern part of the state early. We took fifth out of twenty teams. We took first at our home tournament. They were beginning to think they could. After two more overnight tournaments, we thought we were as ready for the state tournament as we were going to get. A team on the western part of the state that was a contender every year took notice of us. Their coach wanted us to come to his dual-meet tournament so that he could get a look at us. We told them that we had gone to three overnight tournaments and didn't believe we could tax our wrestlers to kick in for another. The coach said that he knew of a hunting camp where we could spend the night, so we agreed to go. We went, spent the night at the hunting camp, and then spat in the face of their hospitality by winning the tournament. After that, our guys decided that they could. We ended up taking second in state that year, which was by far our best effort.

Denise started making more and more enemies. She usually compounded her problems by reacting incorrectly. She began to act like she was the only person that could solve our problems. The kicker for her was the incident with the football players. One the football stars was built like a brick shithouse. His house caught fire and burned down. Denise thought that she could help out, so one evening, she took him and three other young, black football stars to Walmart to buy some stuff. That may not sound like a bad thing, but you would have to think about it in a different way to see what was wrong. If I decided to take three attractive teenage girls shopping, I would be putting myself into a situation that could be detrimental to my career. I know that because I am a male, and since males have one thing on their mind, I am asking for trouble by going anywhere with teenage girls. All a girl has to say is that I tried, and then I'm guilty unless I can prove otherwise.

The football players didn't complain, but Denise had enough enemies that would. This incident wasn't enough by itself to get her fired; however, the complaints about her were piling up. She had accomplished their goal. She had cleared out some of the dead weight. The mentality that she had developed to accomplish this was coming back to smack her in the face. The harsh atmosphere that she had fostered was no longer needed. As I said earlier, I'm not sure she wasn't sacrificed from the beginning.

Principals are not fired when they don't work out. They are given a different job. She was told at the end of the year that she was going to take over the online classes. The online classes were for students that had failed classes and didn't want to take them again. It was especially convenient to seniors who failed a first semester class but wanted to graduate that year.

Denise became the example of the educational corollary to the Peter's Principle. She was too ditzy to be a good math teacher, so she became an administrator. When she wasn't working out as an assistant principal, they made her a principal. When she didn't work out as a principal, they made a job in the central office for her. She rose above the level of her incompetence, which is the education corollary to the Peter's Principle.

Denise gave one more emotional speech to the faculty on the last day of school. She cried and blamed her enemies for spreading lies about her. Most of the staff got satisfaction out of her emotional outburst but were also ticked off that she felt she needed to blame everyone else to the very end. There were a couple of teachers that were upset about losing her. I didn't have much of an opinion about it. She didn't bother me, and some of the faculty thought I had kissed her ass to get my preferential treatment. That ticked me off, but I knew that it wouldn't do me any good to argue with them about it.

I also knew that if she had stayed, she would have turned on me. It was her nature. I have a knack for saying too much, and eventually, I would say the wrong thing. I guess the moral of the story is like in the poem. The old "If you don't like the way I do it" mentality in an educational or government environment can backfire on you.

MY AFFAIR WITH KATRINA

As I lay awake that first night after the "super hurricane" hit, I was thinking that my life had been cruising along in a groove that some might start to think of as a rut. When a person does the same thing day after day, no matter whether he likes it or not, no matter if he thinks he's good at it or not, it begins to feel like a rut. Today was different. This was not a run-of-the-mill experience. This was an adventure. This day, I had seen up close what most of the nation was watching on the news, and this adventure was just starting.

Earlier in the morning, I was standing at the back sliding-glass door watching as the wind came off the roof of the house right behind us. The wind was not coming from directly east, but slightly north of east. I was totally absorbed in watching a tree in my neighbor's yard, which was two feet in diameter and maybe a hundred feet tall, leaning heavily on another. I just knew the second tree was not going to hold up the falling tree. It was straining terribly from the weight. That tree was going down, and it would cause quite a bit of damage when it did. There were fences, sheds, and houses within its reach. In fact, it might bring the other tree with it. I didn't get to see it go, though. I was preoccupied with the events of that day.

It was August 28, 2005, and this day was headed toward becoming a significant one for me and for thousands of others. A category-five hurricane was taking up most of the Gulf. It was cocked and aimed right for us. Her name was Katrina, and she was definitely showing her ugly side.

My story isn't anything special. I didn't spend that day clinging to life, and I wasn't a hero for saving anybody or anything. This is just a story about what my family, friends, and I went through in the process of coming back from a "super hurricane."

One day, about a week after that crazy Katrina came cruising by, I was a couple of blocks down the street watching a utility crew replace an old pole with a new one. Utility companies from possibly a third of the country had sent crews down to Louisiana and Mississippi to help put us back together. Within a couple days of the storm, the entire parking lot of our biggest mall was completely filled with white, yellow, red, green, and blue large utility trucks. They set up a multitude of tents for this army of people for eating, sleeping, and personal needs, like showering.

While the reports coming from New Orleans were of people shooting at rescuers and looting, on the Northshore, we lived by one uncontested rule. It wasn't a complicated rule, and it wasn't even talked about much. It was just one of those truths that everyone knew: utility trucks *always* have the right of way.

The crew I was watching that September morn was from Omaha. Since I was just standing there watching them like I had nothing else to do, a little conversation developed. So I asked them, "Have you ever seen anything as bad as this?" I was pretty sure of the answer when I asked it. What the six-foot-three man with fairly long, grayish-blond hair and a big handlebar mustache said summed things up quite adequately.

"I've been sent into areas after ice storms, snowstorms, and tornadoes, but I've never seen this kind of damage go on for mile after mile after mile."

The first time I heard of Katrina was on Saturday. I was having a yard sale. Jonnie told me that she had made reservations at a hotel in Dallas and asked me if I was coming with them. In a moment of logic and clarity, I formed an opinion that rings of truth to this day. "Oh, hell, it's going to blow off to the east. It always does. If it does go far enough to the west to actually come over us, it won't be much after it travels over all that land." Anybody who spends thirty years down here can claim to know enough about the subject of hurricanes to be a prophetic genius. Let's be fair. Thirty or fifty years ago, all that land would have made a difference, but with all the coastal erosion, there wasn't much land to wear a hurricane down. I am going to have to admit that I made the decision to stay without even looking at the news.

Jonnie, my daughters Amber and Molly, Dan (Molly's husband), Carlton, and Emma (my grandkids) were leaving early in the morning to go to Dallas. There were at least 100,000 people leaving the area that day. Traffic leading to areas of safety was horrendous. Luckily, the region had had a dress rehearsal when another hurricane was headed our way earlier in the hurricane season. A lot of cars had gotten stuck on the interstate leaving town that time and spent hours going nowhere. A lot of the people who stayed this time decided to do so based on the experiences from the previous disaster. This time, a lot more people avoided the interstate.

David, my son, was staying in his house with his family about a mile away from me. Our two dogs and Molly's dog were staying with me.

I sold a couch and a box spring/mattress set at the yard sale on Saturday, but the people never came and got them. I stored them under my carport and covered them up with tarps. I spent Sunday mowing the yard, weed-eating the ditches, and putting everything in the garden and on the porch away. Jackie never understood why I would mow the yard and weed-eat the ditches when a storm was coming to mess everything up. I learned from one of the near misses in the past that the yard is much easier to clean if the grass is cut short, and the water flows better with a clear ditch. I also had to put plywood over the windows. The two windows that I did not cover were the windows on the north side. That was a tactical error, for sure. The north wind pushed my neighbor's trees through those two windows.

On Sunday morning, I went looking for a place that was open to get a can of tobacco, which is my only vice, besides some others, and only found one gas station open. The attendant said they were closing at noon. The streets were full of vehicles packed and heading out of town.

I'm not sure what it was that made it feel like everybody was evacuating the area, but I could just feel it. All traffic was heading out of town.

On Sunday night, I let the dogs out and settled down in my recliner in the living room. I fell asleep and woke up about five. Not ten minutes after I woke up, the lights went out. I let the dogs in. It was deathly quiet. Well maybe not deathly quiet, because I'm not sure what deathly quiet is. Let's try it again. It was really, really quiet. That's not very good either, is it? I was in the middle of a town of thirty thousand, and I didn't hear a car, a dog, or sirens. The only thing you could hear was the wind blowing gently through the treetops. *Gently* was the part that surprised me. It seemed like it should be blowing harder. It was eerie. It had the feel of impending disaster.

I went back to sleep for a couple of hours. By then, the wind had picked up. I ate breakfast and watched. I left half of one of my two sliding glass doors uncovered with plywood, and I spent a lot of time looking out the back door to the east. The way the wind whipped off the roof in back of me was how I could tell which way the wind was coming from. When it got to whipping pretty good, the wind was coming from the east-northeast. As it went on, it started coming more from the north.

I was on my cell phone with my son when the damn thing went out. I hadn't gotten to finish describing to him the tree that was falling. If I would have known that there were hundreds of trees going down all over the place, I would have been more scared.

About 10:30 or 11:00, I decided that it was a good time for a sandwich. Just as I got the sandwich made, I heard a pretty loud thump on the roof. I looked out the kitchen window and could barely see that a tree was spanning the distance between the shed on the northeast corner of the lot and the house. The shed looked messed up, but I couldn't really make out how much damage there was.

Not long after that, maybe even while I had the same sandwich, I heard a crash in my office, which is on the north side of the house. A tree from my neighbor's yard had gone through the window. The wind and the water were pouring in. Luckily, I had put all the computers, including the one in my office, in the laundry room on top of the washing machine. I looked in a nearby closet to see if I could find anything to cover the window with. All I saw was a tablecloth that was plastic on one side and had fuzzy cotton backing on the other. I was somewhat prepared to handle the problems of the day, considering it was my first "super hurricane." I had charged the batteries to my combination drill, small circular saw, and Craftsman flashlight set the day before.

I climbed up to try and screw the tablecloth to the window. Of course, when I tried to screw the tablecloth to the trim, it would just twist up and not penetrate. I knew of some wood strips under the carport, so I headed out to get them. I went out the back door, where I discovered about three or four inches of water. I waded through the water toward the carport. Just as I got to the carport, a huge limb fell behind me, about two feet from where I had just been standing. It wasn't big enough to kill me, but it would have been big enough to knock me out. I had a brief image of me drowning in my backyard in three inches of water because I got knocked out by a limb; however, I didn't have time to dwell on my brush with doom, so I grabbed the strips and headed back to cover the window. By the time I covered the window, the carpet was soaked. I didn't look in the other room on the north side, but trees had knocked out that window also.

A few years earlier, Allison, another hurricane, had spent about a week offshore spreading about twenty inches of rain over the area in a week. One night, it was storming like hell. In the middle of the night, my daughter came and woke me up because she smelled gas. When I went to investigate, I found about six inches of water in the backyard, and it was quiet. I realized that I had left a gas can on top of a cooler and that it had spilled. While I was out there, I cleaned out the drainage hole by the fence and went back to bed. Not long after I got back into bed, it started to storm again, complete with blowing winds and debris falling on the roof. It turns out that I had been standing in the eye of the storm. I felt cheated. I had been in my first eye of a tropical storm and didn't realize it. I wanted to see and observe the eye of a big storm. Well, I was about to get my wish.

About noon or one o'clock, the winds started to die down. Finally, it became very quiet. I went out front and looked around. We were catching the western edge of the eye. I didn't see any blue sky, which is what I'd heard that you can see. The landscape was a disaster. Water covered the street and half my driveway. The trees in the vacant lot across the street were just skeletons with all the branches stripped off. Limbs, leaves, and trash were everywhere. I took a few pictures with an outdated digital camera. Our good digital camera was in Dallas. Soon after I went back in the house, the wind started to pick up again, exclusively from the north.

At one point during the storm, I decided to go up to the front part of the house for something. As I went through the door separating the two parts of the house, I could hear a phone ringing. It was the landline. By the time I picked up the phone, the caller had hung up, but I could hear the dial tone. I unplugged it from the wall and took it back to the part of the house where I was staying and plugged it in. It was the only communication device I had. Later, it rang again. Surprise, it was David. Even though we had no cell phones, the landline was working on a limited basis. I couldn't get outside of a small area like the other side of the interstate, but it helped me stay in touch with the only other member of my family still in the area.

On the back part of the storm, I fell asleep for a while. It's a good thing I didn't know how many big trees were falling over and tearing up everything. A lot of houses were crushed by big trees. The trees seemed to go down in two ways. About half of them just blew over, exposing a huge root ball. The small trees didn't do that. The little ones were flexible enough to bend with the wind. It was the biggest, fullest trees that blew over. A huge tree from two yards over fell on my shed after that first tree hit it. Between the two of them, they pretty well smashed my shed.

The other half of the trees that went down broke off about halfway up. I think that when the wind goes blowing through a group of trees at almost two hundred miles an hour, it creates mini tornadoes that twist and break the trees about halfway up. My neighbor to the north's trees took a hell of a beating. His trees were the closest trees to a main thoroughfare, so they were the ones that took the brunt of the winds whipping down the open street. I lost only one of my trees, and it fell in my south-side neighbor's yard. Most of the damage to my yard was caused by my neighbor's trees to the east and north. My backyard was filled with neighbor's trees. I wouldn't, or couldn't, have slept if I had known about the trees. I know, you're wondering why I didn't know that. Give me a break. It was my first "super hurricane."

When I woke up about four, most of the storm had passed. There was still some wind blowing through the tops of the trees. I went out the front to survey the damage. I was afraid to step into the water. I pictured some power line lying in the water, waiting for me to step in it. The neighbors two houses down had stayed, and their kids were wading through the water, so I figured I could do it. If you get caught in a "super hurricane," make sure you have some children around to test out the water for you.

When I got to the street, I was standing in water that was up to the middle of my calves. I talked to the neighbor kids for a little while. I looked around and couldn't help but think that a bomb had gone off. Trees were lying across the streets in all directions. The ones that were still standing were just a fraction of their former selves.

I walked the half block to the main thoroughfare. The street usually flooded every time it rained three or four inches. The water was up to my mid thigh when I stepped off the curb. I walked east about two blocks and turned south for a block. That was Eleventh Street, which had to be the high ground for the entire area. It was high and dry. It didn't even get covered in water. The big hospital for the area was on the two blocks east of that one. I figured that was important. Since we were close to the hospital, hopefully, we would be one of the first areas to have electricity restored. I came back by way of Florida Street.

Earlier that day, I had heard someone on the radio predict that we were going to have about two or three weeks of no electricity. At the time, I considered that unimaginable. However, when I got to Florida Street, I began to wonder if it was possible to have electricity that soon. A pole on the corner of Florida and Eleventh was snapped halfway up, and a gas line across the street was torn away from the meter and spewing gas. The power line on Florida Street had three huge trees draped across it. It looked mighty obvious that all the structure for delivering electricity had to be replaced.

I had to climb in and around a bunch of trees on my way home. I saw a few people walking around, and we talked some. I do believe that we were all a bit shell-shocked. We were walking around in some sort of daze.

When I got back home, I made a trip around the house. I took some big cutters with me, but it still took me about a half hour to cut a path around the house. There were a lot of trees in the way.

After I was home awhile, my legs began to itch, as if I was having an allergic reaction. I have no idea what was in the water in the street. The faucet water had stopped about ten or eleven o'clock, so I couldn't wash my legs off. I went to the medicine cabinet looking for some Benedryl or something. As I was putting it on, I heard a small drip come out of the faucet. A leap of hope quickly developed. I went over to the faucet and turned it on. Water came out. Hallelujah! It wasn't coming out very hard, but it was coming out. I quickly jumped into the shower, since I didn't know how long it would last. It was one of those good showers. No two showers are alike. Some are better than others. That one was up there on the list. It's probably a top ten, maybe five.

That night was extremely still. Considering how hard it had been blowing earlier, there wasn't a breath of wind that night. It was hot and muggy and still. I didn't have a generator, but you could hear Tom's generator two doors down. Occasionally, you would hear a siren. When I stood outside, it felt like most of the people in the town were gone. Imagine that.

I don't think I slept much that first night. It was stifling. That's not a word that I use often, but if you think of no wind when you say *stifling,* then we're good. If you are thinking *humid* when you say *stifling,* then we're still good. If *too quiet* has a way of adding to your concept of *stifling,* I'd say that that did indeed add to the general feel of stifling.

Day Two: It took me an hour to get the driveway clean enough to get Molly's car out into the street. It's amazing that the car didn't get hit with a single branch. Because David had my chainsaw and I needed it, I headed over to his house. The metal roof to the fairly large apartment complex around the corner was all over Gause Street, which was the main street in town. Even though Gause had had water up to the middle of my thigh the day before, it was dry in the morning. I went east for two blocks and turned north onto Robert Boulevard. I went a block on Robert and ran into a spider web of power lines. All five lanes were blocked, so I had to go over a block beside the high school and then back onto Robert a block down.

When I got down to the street leading into David's subdivision, it was blocked off by a downed tree. I pulled over to the side and was going to walk back when I noticed a small pickup coming out to the left. I pulled over to the tree and went through. Good thing there wasn't a lot of traffic. As I drove back, I could tell that some people had already gotten out their chainsaws and started to cut away what was in the way.

David had gotten about six inches of water in his house. All the carpeting, clothing, and books that were on the floor in the house were no good anymore. We didn't try to do all the cleaning up at once. While I was there, I helped them tear out the carpet and the first foot of sheetrock on the walls of the living room. When David moved into that house, he'd had to replace the bottom twelve inches of his sheetrock because of

Allison. He already knew that it had a propensity to flood. For now, we were just cutting up to the previous joint.

His house flooded because of backed-up runoff. The water wasn't that nasty to clean up. All the houses that flooded on the south side of town, near the lake, had a varying layer of thick, black, smelly crap otherwise known as mud covering the yard, house, and anything else around. Everything that was on the floor when you left was covered in the closest impression of feces that I believe I've ever seen when you got back. After we got everything cleared out of the living room, they made sure it got plenty of fan action. He didn't have to worry so much about the dreaded mold, but it was the great fear that everyone had to deal with.

While I was there, I got my chainsaw. He didn't need it. He had no trees down that made any difference. He said that he couldn't get it to start. I took it and started it right up. You just had to know how to do it. I told David I was going to check on his uncle, Jackie's brother. I hadn't heard from him since Sunday.

When I got back to Robert Drive, I took a left instead of a right, which would have taken me home, and went over the overpass across Interstate 12. As I got over the interstate, I tried going left on the street running alongside the interstate, but I ran into another power-line spider web. I had to go through a gas station driveway to get down that road. I ran by my brother-in-law Joe's house, but he wasn't there, and there was nothing telling me where he had gone. It was two days before I found out where he was.

I left and went back to the overpass to go home, but there was now a cop who said I couldn't go over that bridge. Nobody was stopping me when I went over it the first time. I told him that I lived near Gause Street and that I had just been across that bridge, but he said I would have to go around. So get this: I had to go about two miles east, four miles south, and three miles west just to get back, which was only about two miles from where I started. When I got up to the intersection of

Interstate 10 and Gause, a second cop stopped me and asked me where I was going, so I told him. He said all right and sent me on. About twenty yards farther, a third cop stopped me. I was beginning to get the feeling that the authority figures called the police were at a loss as to what they should be doing. Give them a break. It was their first "super hurricane."

The last cop who stopped me was a former student of mine, as was his sister. I felt like I needed to vent, so I went into a tirade as to how I had to go all the way around. I finished it off with the question, "What was the point of all that?"

To which he replied, "Because it was you." It made sense. Now that I knew why, I could let go of all the hostilities, so I went on my merry way.

At home, I took out my chainsaw and decided to cut up some of the trees that were blocking the street on my block. I got one tree cut up and moved off the street when two brothers came walking down the street. They came over and asked if they could borrow my chainsaw to get someone out that was blocked in by some fallen trees. I told them they had to take me with them, if they wanted to use my chainsaw. Since I don't have any friends, that's the way I get to go with people. I set conditions so that I get included. Actually, I probably didn't trust them.

We walked about three blocks over. We, of course, had to weave in and out of trees and went by another leaking gas meter to get there. The street we wanted to clear was blocked by two trees and a pole. We cut about eight feet out of the middle of each. The trees weren't hard. It was the pole that was tricky because of all the wires and stuff. There were about six guys around to help, and all we needed to cut out was about eight feet, so it didn't take long. It was a real bonding thing for me, but none of them have called or come by since then. Maybe the emotions were one-sided. Once those people got past these three obstacles, they had an open road up to Eighth Street. Eighth Street had been cleared out first thing that morning because the local government president lived on Eighth Street, and they wanted him out and about.

When I got back to my block, I was getting tired, but there were still small trees blocking the street. So I cut them up, but I didn't move them off the street. I felt like I had done enough for that day. It's a good thing too. By the time I got down to my house, along came a backhoe that used his bucket to clear the street a lot quicker than I would have.

I called David when I got home and asked him if he was coming over. We had discussed it earlier. I had a gas grill with propane, and I had meat in the freezer to get rid of before it went bad. I told them I had ribs and chicken. It turns out that I had convinced them to come over when Wanda, David's wife, found out I had ribs. She loves ribs.

David brought over a generator. It belonged to Wanda's sister, and she wasn't using it because she was staying with her father. I was only going to get to use it for a little while because they wanted it back. Later, he called me and told me I could keep it because they decided that they didn't need it. So that night, there were two generators disturbing the peace in that neighborhood. I plugged in the refrigerator, the freezer, and a fan. It was a lot nicer with a fan. And that was Tuesday.

Day Three: I went back over to David's on Wednesday, and we cleaned out the bedroom. We gave it the same treatment as before with the living room. That took us a couple of hours, and then we went out back for a while and talked. I said that I needed to go to Baton Rouge on Thursday. David was thinking the same thing, so we agreed to go together the next day. We needed to go to Baton Rouge, because that was how far we had to go to get reception on our cell phones. We also had to get some supplies, including gas, and Baton Rouge was the nearest place with open stores. Baton Rouge is about ninety miles away. I wanted something else to cook on, and I needed some more propane. There were lots of little things we needed, like rope, clothespins, and a few tools.

Before I went to Baton Rouge, I needed to go look at a few houses so that I could call some people and let them know how their properties were doing. Jonnie and the rest had not yet heard from us. They had no idea what was going on. The news was not telling them much. Most of what they heard was about New Orleans and that it was in total breakdown. The only thing they said about the Northshore was that it was wiped out.

I went over to Molly's house first. On Tuesday, they wouldn't let me past Fremeaux because of the flooding. Old town still had six feet of water. David was taking some sort of fluids class at the University of New Orleans that semester. It was probably a physics class, like maybe wave dynamics. He calculated based off of what he had heard, the storm surge was going to penetrate five miles inland. It was part of why he decided to stay. Fremeaux was that five-mile point inland, and that's where the flooding stopped. Now, I didn't actually see these calculations that David said he'd seen, so it's entirely possible that he made all that crap up just to impress me. I'm guessing that was the case.

On Wednesday, they wouldn't let me go down First Street, but I could go on Third Street, even though it still had a few inches on it. I parked for a moment, wondering if I should drive through the water or if I should walk. While I was thinking about it, a black guy came up and introduced himself to me. After a short conversation, he was tagging along with me. He knew where the police would let me go, and he looked eager to go. I think he just wanted to kill some time. I figure if he had anything to do, I wouldn't have been able to talk him into it. I also thought that maybe I could use the help.

We went up two blocks on Third Street, through the water, and then turned right and went two blocks to Front Street. I'm glad I drove, because it would have been a long walk to Molly's house. I drove down Front Street, around the curve to Old Spanish Trail. When I got to Molly's street, it was blocked off with trees, so I walked two blocks to her house. I didn't try to go in. I could tell by the water marks on the house that she had had six feet of water in the house. I headed back home, but first I dropped Earl or Homer or whatever the black guy's name was back off at his hotel and gave him a few dollars. I didn't have much to give.

After we ate, I went back down to the south side to find out what happened to Jackie's sister Jenny's house to see what had happened to it. I couldn't get down her street, so I parked and walked. I didn't actually see her house, because I would have had to go another three blocks, but I did see her neighbor across the street. He said she got about seven or eight feet of water in her house. While I was in the neighborhood, I went over to check out Chip's house. Chip was my assistant wrestling coach and had gone to Houston with his family. I talked to Chip's neighbor across the street, and he let me know that Chip got about three feet in the house.

That night, between cleaning out the car for the trip the next day and trying to sleep in the car because it was too hot in the house, I made some noise opening and closing the doors. From two doors down, Tom came over to see if everything was going all right. Since we were the only people staying in the neighborhood, I think he thought, like me, that we needed to keep an eye on the neighborhood. He had heard that there was looting going on at the outlet mall. I sort of accepted the looting rumor at the time, but there was something gnawing at my brain. The first thing that bugged me was that there was nothing to loot at the outlet mall. It was supposed to be this great development that was going to make a lot of money for the town in the eighties. However, it didn't take long for the companies to bail out of their retail outlet stores. Within ten to fifteen years, it was dead. By the time Katrina came to pay us a visit, that sad shopping center only had the pottery store renting anything.

The second thing about that statement was disinformation that was spread with the rumor. A few of the rumors that went around revolved around the word *gone*. I heard Grand Isle was gone; Chalmette High was gone; Eden Isle was gone; and, of course, the twin spans were gone. Now, each of these statements had a varying degree of truth to them, but the term *gone* had a broad range lying inside its definition. So, let me advise you that the next time you are in a "super hurricane," make sure you don't believe everything you hear.

I was trying to save the gas for the generator when I tried to sleep in the car. It was a lousy place to sleep. It would be cool while the car was running, but it quickly got hot and muggy when you turned it off. I figured it wasn't a good idea to sleep in a running car all night, so I gave up and went back inside. I didn't run the generator, so it was a miserable night.

Day Four: Originally, we were going to take two cars to Baton Rouge, but we ended up just taking one. We got off at the exit that had an IHOP and a Walmart. The first thing I did was call Jonnie, and then I called my mom. As I said earlier, they hadn't heard any news from the area since early on Monday. It was now Thursday. People that were out of town didn't know if they were allowed to come back or even it there was anything to come back to. The news out of the area was telling everybody that the authorities were not letting people come back. I don't think anybody thought that there would be such a total disruption in everybody's life in such a big area for so long. Jonnie had moved the group to Houston. They got the rooms in Houston cheaper. While we were on the phone, Jonnie decided to come back on Saturday. Dan, Molly's husband, wanted me to go look through his house for his dad's bass guitar, which was about the only thing he had from his real dad.

After I called Jonnie, I called my mom. She hadn't been happy about me staying when I talked to her on Sunday. Of course, four days without any news was very stressful for her. Hearing from me lightened the stress load, but it didn't relieve all of it.

I called Jenny while I was there. She'd already heard news on her house, but I found out that fourteen different people were staying at her son's house near Baton Rouge, which pretty well accounted for everybody that was missing.

I also called Chip. They had heard about their house, but they hadn't heard from an uncle of hers in Mississippi. I said I would see what I could find out if they told me how to find him. Later, I went out and tried to find him, but I never did. It was a long shot.

David, Wanda, and I felt like IHOP would be a nice treat while we were there. I think we just felt like since we had been roughing it, it would be nice to sit and have a nice breakfast while we were in civilization. We saw some news people outside of IHOP who were asking some questions about where we were from and what the situation was like there. I don't know where they were from, but I could tell they were just getting into the area. I tried to tell them that I personally saved thousands of people, but I don't think they bought it. That was probably the best chance I had for fame and fortune.

David and Wanda bought a bunch of stuff from Walmart. I tried to buy a stove, but they didn't have any. I did buy a propane tank and some rope. After we left Walmart, we got propane for my tank and gas for the car. We filled up about four or five five-gallon cans.

After we got back and put up a few things, David and I took a ride toward the south side. The first place we headed was to Molly's. I had a key to get in, and we thought we would look around for the guitar. We had brought the chainsaw, and we were going to cut a hole through the trees so that we could get back to her house. We were doing good until we hit a tree that had a strange force direction. I know. I just made up that term, so how would you know what I'm talking about? Normally, if a log is supported on the ends, you don't want to cut down in the middle or the chain will bind, and bound chains are how you get hurt. Usually, you can cut it down, if you make the cut real wide and wedge-shaped. If I would have been cutting down on that log, things would have gone fine, but this time, David convinced me that I should be cutting up. As I started cutting it up, the tree started shifting up and bound up the chain. I cut off the engine in a hurry. It turns out that the ball to that tree was acting like a counterweight and making the middle of the tree want to go up. As soon as I weakened it, it went up. We had a hard time, but we finally got the blade out of the tree. We walked the two blocks to the house.

I opened the door to the house. The water and objects left a strange pattern inside. It was circular, as if everything that could float bobbed around like it was going down the toilet and then fell wherever it was when the water left. Nothing was standing inside. We found the guitar, but the case was shot and falling apart. We just left the case outside in the yard and took the guitar. There wasn't any reason to do it, but I locked the door when we left.

As we were walking back to the car, about a block from Molly's house, we saw a dog inside a four-foot fence. There didn't seem to be any indication that the owners had been there all week. I wondered what that dog had done to survive the storm. Obviously, it had found some high ground, because the water had gotten higher than the fence in that area. He was too wound up to let us pet him or do anything with him. I wonder what happened to him.

Next, we went toward Eden Isles, where my sister-in-law and brother-in-law lived. When we got to the part of Highway 11 that ran along that canal that was in *Live and Let Die,* they wouldn't let us go any farther. All the houses on the canal side were gone. There's that word again. They weren't totally gone, but they had no value. The waves had got up under them and just busted them up. Gatemouth Brown, who is a local jazz legend, had a house along that highway that got busted up. I hear he never really got over it. He spent his last year in Texas, of all places. We went toward Interstate 10 on Oak Harbor Drive, which went along the golf course and the newer—and, in my opinion, more pretentious—part of Eden Isles. There was all sorts of junk on the levees. There was a huge bundle of two-by-fours, a dumpster, all sorts of wood, and, of course, trash.

We went by Karren's house. Turns out they had gone to Memphis to get hotel rooms, which I found that out that morning when I talked to Jenny. They only got about four feet of water, even though their lot faces the open water. It just sits up fairly high off the water. When they developed Eden Isles out of a shrimp estuary, they piled the mud that was dug out to make the waterfronts on the side to build off of. This left most of the houses in Eden Isles on high ground. We couldn't get back to Terry's house, because the sludge that covered everything around there had not dried out enough for us to drive on. Terry was Jonnie's brother. Turns out Terry's house had two drums of hazardous materials deposited on his back porch and in his living room, not to mention a ton of trash, like the remnants of docks that had been busted up by the storm.

We went back toward the interstate. First we went back by the marina. We didn't get too far because of all the mud, but we got far enough back that way to see a forty-foot sailboat and about a fifty-foot barge on the side of the street. It was odd to see them sitting there at least a hundred yards from the water.

As we went home, there were several boats on the interstate. I recognized one of them as Larry's; it was upside down in between the eastbound and westbound lanes of the interstate. I worked for Larry, a boat builder, for twelve years. His yard was on the west side of the interstate in between Eden Isles and Old Spanish Trail. Further down was a houseboat. I still see that houseboat in a yard along the Frontage Road on the east side of the interstate.

Day Five: I had heard that the Sam's store out by the mall had gas to sell. You had to admire the businesses that made an effort to get back up and running. I heard that you had to get there early because it ran out early. I tried to get up about 6:00, but since I didn't have an alarm clock, I didn't make it up until 6:30. By the time I got out there, the line was over two blocks long. I didn't wait; I left.

Later, a couple of friends of Dan's came by in almost a hysterical state asking if I had seen his dad's guitar. I told them I had it, and they sighed in great relief. It seems that they had gone by the house and found the case thrown on the ground but no guitar. That's because I took it.

The only other thing that was of any interest on Friday happened at about eight or nine o'clock that night, when a convoy of trucks carrying pontoons came down Main Street and stopped for a while. I don't know what they had in mind for those pontoons, but I'm guessing they were going toward the only bridge open to New Orleans, which was the Highway 11 bridge. Being as there were no streetlights and there was nothing going on, it was sort of exciting. It's amazing how exciting something can be when there's nothing going on.

When I got back to the house, Chip was there. He was on his way back to check out his house, and he brought me a little present of some gas. Everyone needed gas at that time. Jenny's husband had brought me some from Baton Rouge, but I could always use more. What I had would run my generator for two days.

Day Six: Jonnie came back the next day. She had left with the van and the convertible. My mom had sent Jackie about fifteen hundred dollars, which was sort of a bad idea. She proceeded to buy an unbelievable amount of crap. She bought at least twice as much as we needed: candles, sterno, cooking fuel, batteries, and general hurricane supplies. She bought a camping stove, which was a good idea, but then she bought five times too much fuel. She bought an air conditioner, which I thought was a terrible idea, but it turned out to be a good one. It was nice to sleep in one cool room.

We spent the last few days with a routine. We spent our evenings in the back cooking and eating what was in the freezer. We understood that we didn't have all our creature comforts, but we had resigned ourselves to living the best we could with what we had. The problem was that Jonnie didn't want to live with what she had. She didn't want to eat outside. She wanted to have air conditioning. She had bought a small air conditioner and wanted to live in comfort. I wasn't too ready to put up with prima donna crap. I was very pissed off that she had bought so much and that she wasn't being flexible to the situation. I didn't set up the air conditioner that night, but I did the next day. I wasn't in the mood to do it because 1) it wasn't what I had my mind set on; and 2) because I wasn't sure how well the generator was going to be able to handle the refrigerator, the freezer, and an air conditioner. It turns out, the air conditioner felt so good at night that I soon lost my passion toward not wanting it.

The next day was about where the blur began. The streets began to get more crowded as more people began to return to their houses. We started hearing about help stations where you could get water or ice. There was one place where you could get a hot meal every day, but I didn't need the hot meal so much because I had a grill and a lot of meat that needed to be eaten. There were also some places that you could get some staples, like water. We couldn't drink the tap water for at least two weeks because of those few hours when the water was shut off. I guess they made a science out of making sure water was safe to drink, and I also guess that's against the rules.

Before Electricity: There are events that help you gauge time. We didn't have electricity for three weeks. For weeks, we went through a daily routine of getting the gas cans together and going find some gas. At first, finding gas wasn't easy and was usually time-consuming. Every time another gas station opened, it decreased the time you waited in line. I still make sure I give the Shell Station on Highway 11 some of my business because they made a good effort to get back open.

I also had to find a way of getting rid of trash. My pile was getting pretty large after awhile. The trash trucks weren't running at first, so I had to find a dumpster. I finally found one near Winn-Dixie that wasn't full. I don't know how long my trash sat there before it got picked up, but at least it wasn't taking up space under my carport.

During that time, I spent a lot of time hauling leaves, branches, and logs to the front and depositing them on the street. Trucks and small loaders ran through the streets picking up yard trash every couple of weeks or so. Some of the streets were hard to get down because of huge piles of limbs and debris on both sides of the street. One day, I noticed that Jackie had a bunch of scratches on the right side of the car. She said she didn't know how they got there, but I did. The little job of cleaning the yard had to take me at least three weeks. My backyard was so full of trees. All of them came from my neighbors. Two huge trees destroyed one of my sheds. Two trees were heading straight for the shed I had worked on all summer, but became wedged in between two other trees just shy of landing on the shed. No big branches hit my pool. I had a four-and-a-half-foot deep by eighteen-foot diameter, round, above-ground pool. A whole bunch of crap got into it, but no branches hit the sides. One tree fell right in between the pool and the good shed. So I guess things could have been worse.

So many people around us had to deal with the process of gutting their houses. To get an idea of what it was like, look around your house and imagine everything you see all piled up out by the curb waiting for loaders and trucks to haul it away. Don't worry about stains on the mattresses or the condition of the furniture, because it was all going out to the curb for everyone to see. It didn't matter whether it was a souvenir from a trip, a momento of a good time, or if it had sentimental value, it was going out by the curb. Everything down to bare studs, including sheetrock, was thrown out. Now, if you can imagine most of the houses on your street with their possessions out by the curb, then you can imagine most of the neighborhoods on the south side of town. My daughter, two of my sisters-in-law, my brother-in-law, and a lot of people I knew all went through that.

Jenny found a crew of Mexicans that could strip her house of everything on the floor and all the sheetrock on the walls. Jenny is a junk-a-holic. I am lucky if I can find a nail clipper or tweezers when I need them, but she had six or seven manicuring sets in each bathroom. She had about eight coffee makers that all worked. She called it her coffee maker collection. Every nook and cranny in the house had to have something in it. So when she was taking all her possessions out to the curb, it was a big pile. She loved her possessions. They were her security blanket. They really meant something to her.

I was there to help. The bad part of it was the two to six inches of black, smelly muck that got stirred up from the bottom of the lake and spread across the entire area from the lake five miles in. In a closed-in house, the smell permeated everything. There was a procession of people tromping in and out of every room with all her possessions and dumping them by the curb. She held up pretty well until it was about time to go. Somebody had taken off her front door and thrown it on the pile. She started crying.

"How are we supposed to close up the house if it doesn't have a front door? I can't close up the house. I don't have a front door." The rantings didn't stop there, and they only got worse. She went out, got in the car, and took off. I put the door back on and stayed until the crew left. I went back the next day while they finished up. I didn't see her for two days. She went back to Baton Rouge. She now says that she doesn't even remember going anywhere that day.

Everybody seemed to have a breaking point at one time or another. One day before electricity, I was in the process of doing one of the infinite number of things that I could think of. We had a lot of time off and a lot of small things to do, like cleaning, moving stuff around, and starting the process of going to agencies and calling insurance companies. I made a shelf for the patio. All right, it wasn't high on the list of important things to do, but I was in sort of a pissy mood, and that's what I felt like doing. I was drinking beer until about two o'clock. Jenny was there at some point. She was coming over to our house to wash some of the dishes and anything else she could salvage. She and Tim, her husband, were staying about four different places, and ours was the best place for her to clean up that stuff.

So, anyway, I decided that I wasn't getting drunk enough with beer and thought some brandy would help. I don't drink that much, as a rule. Most of the time, I stuck to beer, because it was easy to control, but every couple of years or so, I like to really tie one on. Anyway, once I started to drink the brandy, it didn't take long to get me lit. Nobody was around at about five in the afternoon when I decided that the best way to get all the trash out of the pool was to get in it. So I took off all my clothes and got in. I know it's a cliché, but I felt free for a little while. Fishing limbs and leaves out of a pool naked is slightly erotic. I know I did get a lot of trash out of the pool.

I might remember vaguely getting out of the pool, but nothing else. I woke up about five a.m. when the generator ran out of gas. I got up and went to refuel the generator. I took turns throwing up and putting the gas in. After blowing chunks a second time, I started the generator and went back to bed. About nine, I got up and went outside to make coffee or something and threw up again. Jenny was there. Oh, yea, I didn't tell you. When I woke up at five, I had underwear on. I didn't put them on, and I don't think Jonnie did it by herself. Jenny looked slightly odd that morning. That was the day we reverted back toward our previous lives. We turned the lights back on. Such joy.

After Electricity: Inevitably, once the electricity was back on, the talk started about going back to work. Ahhhhhh! The first discussion I had with anyone about getting back to work was a couple of days after Katrina. I was talking to the wife of a school board member that lived in the neighborhood.

She said, "There is one school completely demolished on the south side, and some others are in pretty bad shape. I think it's going to take two months." Now, since she was so well connected, I figured I was in for a two-month vacation from kids. Sort of like a two-month snow day. After a week or so, they started saying something about October first. I know. I think I was robbed too. Maybe it's wrong of me for thinking that, since I had only been back a month when Katrina hit; however, once a thought like a two-month snow day sneaks into your mind, only having one month off hurts. It's amazing what people can accomplish once they set their minds to it. I don't think anybody can estimate the fear in an adult mind, when the thought of kids running the streets for two months with nothing to do is rattling around in there. That's why they got it going so quick. I have to admit, that is a creepy thought.

For the last week of September, we went in to school and tried to do whatever we could think of to do. We were getting paid, so they wanted us around. I think it was sort of like inventorying the staff to see who was there and who wasn't. As it was, we did lose a couple of teachers.

Our school had been a shelter for senior citizens. People were sleeping in my classroom. Once we finally go back to our jobs and start taking care of business, everything started to be about taking care of business.

Before I could start cutting out the section of the tree that spanned from the smashed shed to the house and patio roof, I had to call the insurance company, and they put me touch with my adjuster. He was still in Florida from when Katrina went through there. I didn't even know Katrina went through Florida until then. I was pretty oblivious to the whole "super hurricane" thing, until it came knocking on our door. The adjuster said he didn't want me cutting that tree because he couldn't be responsible, but I countered with the fact that I needed it off my roof and you couldn't find a tree cutter that was free right then. He allowed me to cut it. I made sure I had plenty of pictures before I did anything.

Now came the time when you were waiting for your adjuster to come take a look. Nothing could be purchased until the money flowed. I don't think I'll ever have All State Farm insurance because of the way hurricanes are handled. Most insurance companies that aren't mega have to hire outside adjusters for a catastrophe like this. These outside adjusters are paid as a percentage of your settlement. The more money you make, the more money the adjusters make. The mega insurance companies, on the other hand, can afford to have their own adjusters, so they don't pay that well. Those adjusters are paid by the company, so there is no incentive for them to be generous.

My adjuster said no to some things that were little, but yes to the big things. He wouldn't cover a small heater that was in the shed that got demolished, but he gave me a whole new patio roof, when all it had was a dent in the metal and a crack in one of the two-by-fours. My carport was just about gone before Katrina, but I got some money to replace it. I also got a new roof for the entire house. Since I knew how to do the work myself, I actually made a profit off of Katrina. The only thing I didn't do was reroof the house. I'm getting too old for that crap. I let the Mexicans do that.

There were a lot of Mexican crews in town. I knew the guy that owned the company this group of Mexicans worked for. He used to coach track and teach. Though I didn't see him the entire time we were having it roofed, I felt I could trust him. We could have gotten the roof done cheaper by somebody from Kentucky, but we figured there wasn't much of a guarantee with someone from out of town. Before Katrina, you could get your roof done for ninety dollars a square foot. After Katrina, the roof estimate we turned down was $155 a square foot. The one we accepted was $210 a square foot, and we had another bid that was higher.

The money for the roof was well spent. I got a sub at school because I needed to do some repairs before they started. I wanted to put a diverter above the fireplace so that the water wouldn't dead end at the fireplace. I also had to replace a gable rafter, because it had rotted out. I worked my ass off that day to stay ahead of the Mexicans. I counted seventeen of them at one time. As they tore off the old roof and discovered sections of rotted wood, they would show me, and I would fix them. So between replacing rot, getting more material, and repairing that corner, I barely stayed ahead of them. They were done in a day and a half, and they did a good job.

The insurance company paid the mortgage company instead of us. The mortgage company then had a list of procedures that we would have to do to get the money. They also had an inspection at about the midway point. Part of the procedure was that we had to have estimates of labor and materials. Since I was doing the work, I ended up making up an imaginary company with a letterhead so that I could submit estimates for various sections of the work list the insurance adjuster outlined. It was a pain in the ass at first, but after awhile, it was just part of the job. I still have a dent in the metal roof of my patio and a cracked two-by-four.

It's funny how well you remember the firsts. Of course, electricity was a big one. The first gas station to open in the area was a big deal. When the traffic signal where two four-lane streets intersect started working, it may not have been that big of a deal, but it sure was convenient. The first grocery store to open was not only big but nice. Walmart was the first big place to open. They couldn't find enough workers, so every time you went there, you had to wait in line at the checkout for at least forty-five minutes. I never went there without striking up a conversation with my fellow line-waiters. Some of them, I thought, had become solid friends, but they never called. It may have only been a rumor, but I heard of one couple who had met, got married, and divorced while sitting in line at Walmart. Maybe I'm exaggerating.

In the first days after the storm, there were only two radio stations on the airways. One was all Katrina news. There was a second that carried a lot of Katrina news, but also mixed in a few songs to liven things up. One morning after electricity, I had set the radio/alarm clock so that I could get up on time. When the alarm went off, it was the radio station that I had been listening to since the early '70s. I know. Considering all the things that happened after the storm, for me to call up something so insignificant has got to be a big "so what?" The cutting up trees, cleaning the yard, rebuilding fences, replacing the shed and the carport, cleaning the pool, and everything else that I did in the process of getting back to normal tends to become a blur, for lack of a better word. Yet something as minor as a favorite radio station coming on the air leaves a crystal-clear impression on my mind. That's weird, don't you think? I guess it's a marker for the belief that things will get back to normal one little step at a time.

One day, I believe right after we got our electricity back, the phone rang. It was no big deal, right, because it had been working on a limited basis the whole time. Naturally, I thought it was my son, so I picked it up and said in a rude tone, "What do you want?" My family is used to me doing things like that. The guy on the other end apologized for getting the wrong number. I said, "Wait a minute. Where are you calling from?" My suspicions were correct. He was from outside the area. He was from North Carolina, and we proceeded to talk for five minutes about what was going on. I'm not sure, but I imagine that he was trying to get off the line the whole time, but I held him up because I wanted to tell him about my adventure, and he was too polite to hang up. When we hung up, I called my little brother in Colorado because I didn't know how long the phone was going to stay fixed.

Attitudes, attitudes, what about attitudes? I didn't think much about how people were going to react to stressful life, but I do know that I wouldn't have been able to predict it. As far as school was concerned, there was a huge "I don't give a shit" attitude. For example, I would say to them, "If you don't do this worksheet/turn in the project, you'll get a zero."

They would then turn their heads toward me and tilt them a little, sort of like a puppy when he didn't understand. Slowly, their gaze would turn to the wall for a moment and then return to mine and they would say, "Okay." That would be the last I would see of their faces as they slowly returned their gazes to their friends and continued talking about whatever it was, but it wasn't geometry or English or anything intellectual. Everybody seemed to be in some sort of a funk.

Jonnie did not do well with this upheaval of everyday life. She lost her job at a high school across the lake. One day, she cried for a couple of hours because she had driven by an apartment building that had been torn apart and she could see right into someone's closet. She had a hard time dealing with the fact that just anyone could see all their personal possessions. It was probably the straw that broke her back, because you could go down street after street and see furniture and mattresses, and hairdryers, and refrigerators, and clothes, and whatever. Everybody lost something they didn't want to lose. A lot of pictures, Mother's Day cards, report cards, and other personal, irreplaceable objects were of no value ever again.

I wish I would have had a trailer and a barn or warehouse that was empty. I could have picked up a lot of furniture that just needed some repairing. I got a large, round oak table and two oak chairs that survived Katrina. My next-door neighbor worked at Tulane with a guy that only picked up cherry furniture. He had a complete bedroom and cherry dining room set he'd gotten out of the trash after Katrina. There were a lot of people that felt they didn't have the time or experience to refinish any furniture, so a lot of good stuff was thrown out. I took all I was willing to take on.

David did pretty well with the stress. He stood tall and took care of business for a while, but he had his down times. Part of Molly's stress was having to live with David. They spent almost three months together, and Americans don't do well taking on family for an extended amount of time. After all, we're not used to having the entire family live in the same house. At first, the city wouldn't let her have a building permit because they were contemplating making everybody raise their house to a certain height, which would have been most of the houses on the south side. It took awhile, but I think they figured it was just too impractical to accomplish.

By Christmas, they had stripped everything out, gotten a building permit, done the wiring, and put in the insulation. When I got home for Christmas break, I was savoring the idea of having two weeks off. Jonnie told me Molly was going nuts because there was so much to do, and she wanted to get out of David's house bad. Molly had told Jonnie that she didn't think I wanted to help. So I got my tools and went over to her house. I got the ceiling sheetrocked in one of the bedrooms that night and sort of got in the groove for the next day. The next day, I was doing all the cutting and fitting, and everybody else was putting the sheetrock up. There were about five of them. We got the entire back of the house done that day. It was a good day's work. It took a little longer to do the front part because they were changing things up a bit, and that was taking longer. Inside a week's time, the walls were done and sheetrocked, the new front windows were in, and a crew started mudding the walls (covering the joints in the sheetrock with tape and joint compound).

By New Year's, they were finished mudding the sheetrock and getting ready to do the floors. They moved in sometime in January, even though it wasn't finished. Molly and Dan learned a lot about carpentry that year. I believe a lot of people learned some carpentry that year.

Amber dealt with the stress by moving to Colorado for about nine months. Within a few days after getting back from Houston, she went by some friends in Baton Rouge. It wasn't a month before she was living with a friend she'd met online near Denver.

Aaron, Chip's son, had some real anger issues that year in wrestling. He was a junior and a top-notch wrestler. He was quite often getting into fights with his brother. Our team was at a tournament in Baton Rouge, and he was in the semifinals on the center mat. He got sort of a poor decision from possibly the worst ref in the state. Chip just about lost it on that. He became quite toxic to the ref. A second decision came that was worse than the first. As the ref made the decision, he looked right at Chip and smiled, which indicated that he wasn't really trying to do what was right; he just wanted to piss Chip off. Chip had a tendency to inspire people like that. He really went off that time and got himself ejected. Soon after, Aaron quit wrestling with any authority and just defended against his opponent. After a little while, the match was called, and he was ejected from the tournament. John, Aaron's brother, was in the corner after his dad was ejected. John tried to get Aaron to shake hands with his opponent, and they almost got into a fight in front of everybody in the center ring. Afterward, when I told Aaron I wanted to talk to him, he refused. I was quite upset that he had embarrassed our team. Later, we had our talk when he had finally gotten a grip on himself. He came to me and asked what I wanted to talk about. I wasn't too pleased, and I let him know how bad it was.

Aaron's problem came from the fact that he and Mark were staying in a FEMA trailer in the front of the house while they fixed it up. FEMA trailers were travel trailers that the government gave out to families so that they could live nearby while they fixed up their houses. Mark was not a member of the family, but he was Aaron's best friend for about three years. Mark was also a wrestler. Mark's family had moved to Oklahoma after Katrina, and Chip had offered to let him stay with them. The problem was that Chip was very domineering, and there were plenty of bad attitudes going around, because Chip didn't know how to not make a big deal out of everything. Everyone at the place was putting in a couple of evenings fixing the house up. This combined with the general funk that everybody in the region was experiencing and produced a very short temper.

Aaron also liked a freshman girl who was our manager. The girl was John's girlfriend's younger sister. For a little while, they went out, but she decided that she didn't want to be attached to him. He told everyone on the team that he didn't want anybody going out with her, but she was attractive and she drew her share of admirers. The fact that John and Matt were in the same house and had girlfriends did not help.

The Monday following the fiasco at the tournament, Aaron got into another fight with his brother John. I took Aaron outside to talk with him. When Chip came out to see what was wrong, I told him that Aaron was having trouble with his temper and had gotten into a fight with his brother. Chip's reaction was to get mad at Aaron and tell him he couldn't go to the next tournament. So Chip's idea of dealing with Aaron's anger problem was to get mad at him. Sort of ironic, don't you think? Aaron and I talked quite a bit over the next few weeks, and eventually, Aaron went back to being his normal self.

Everyone picked up a bad attitude from time to time. Sometimes it was in the form of anger; sometimes it was in the form of apathy. Sometimes it was just that somebody felt they needed to get drunk. You know, I understand that there are all sorts of people in the world who live every day in worse conditions than we were facing, but when your groove or rut is turned upside down and you spend months just trying to get them back to normal, that is a lot to assimilate. We all did some adjusting.

We still mark time by Katrina. If you know someone who had a baby in 2006, that baby was born a year after Katrina. We had a tree get struck by lightning that had to be cut down, nine months after Katrina. Chip, that pain in the ass, was terminated as a coach and teacher at the school, three years after Katrina.

It's still pretty easy to get someone to tell their story of surviving Katrina. All you have to do is bring the subject up. The stress and frustration that we felt as that first year went by is fading, not in leaps and bounds, but gently as our thoughts dwell less and less on those times.

One of the days when we were sitting on the patio before electricity, Buddy, who is Karren's son, suggested that I carve a big hand with the middle finger extended out of one of the logs in the backyard. The reason that he suggested that was because a few years earlier, I had carved an open hand from a log. So I took a four-foot log that was twenty inches in diameter and started carving on it with my chainsaw. I had sort of quit on the first hand because it looked off proportionally. This time, it was better. I didn't have to use the chisel as much this time. I also used a grinder more. So I now have a three-foot-high hand with all the fingers neatly folded over, except for one large middle finger, with "Katrina" burned into the base below it. I tried to sell it on eBay for $700, but someone from Mexico tried to con me. I was lucky not to have lost anything.

You know, my rut doesn't look like as much of a rut anymore. It looks more like a groove. I had felt for years that my life was dull, but Katrina made me realize that dull ain't that bad.

ABOUT THE AUTHOR

I left the small town that I grew up in when I was eighteen with a desire for adventure. That story is *My Trip to Mardi Gras.* I married the woman I met during that Mardi Gras and had a son when I was twenty. I spent the next fifteen years surviving life and working a variety of jobs while supporting a family (three children and a wife). I worked at two different paint companies, at a lumberyard for three and a half years, for Crazy Charlie doing offshore housing, and at a shipyard on the Mississippi River. I also did renovation work in uptown New Orleans and built fiberglass boats for years. I acquired a wide range of knowledge and skills.

At the tender age of twenty-nine, I enrolled in college and graduated a mere seven years later with a degree in secondary math education. I spent twenty-five years teaching math (mostly geometry) at a small high school in Louisiana. I am recently retired and looking forward to facing another phase of my life.

I have acquired a talent for spewing my own brand of bull in all phases of my life.

ABOUT THE BOOK

The main story of this book is about eight months I spent out on the road in the seventies hitchhiking across the country twice. I also wrote two smaller short stories. "The Rise and Fall of a Dictator" is about teaching at a high school, and "My Affair With Katrina" is about living through a natural disaster.

I know what you're thinking. I know you're tired of reading stories about hitchhiking, teaching, and Katrina. I'll bet that if you had a dollar for all the stories you've read lately about those three subjects, you could retire too. Why can't anyone think up something new, like vampires and zombies?